Square Grouper

A Finn Pilar Key West Mystery

LEWIS C. HASKELL

ABSOLUTELY AMAZING eBOOKS

Published by Whiz Bang LLC, 926 Truman Avenue, Key West, Florida 33040, USA

For information contact:
Publisher@AbsolutelyAmazingEbooks.com

ISBN-13: 978-1519371812
ISBN-10: 1519371810

A special thanks to my wife Susan for her loving support, encouragement and excellent editing. She laughed at the fun parts and mildly erotic ones. What more can a man ask for?

SQUARE GROUPER

CHAPTER ONE

THE SECOND BODY to show up was just off Smathers Beach in Key West, wrapped like a typical *Square Grouper*. That's the local's name for marijuana bales that float in regularly courtesy of smugglers who get spooked by passing Coast Guard patrols and dump their loads overboard.

The bales are usually wrapped in heavy black plastic and float in on the tides along with tangles of rotting kelp that provide a pungent ocean bouquet for the drive along South Roosevelt Blvd. Some enterprising islanders and the occasional homeless resident have been known to collect these bundles for *medicinal use.*

While I live frugally on my modest investments, imagining I am a retired cop instead of one who was 'invited to resign', I still phone in these arrivals to the local Key West PD.

Every morning I ride my rather rusty beach cruiser around the two by four square mile island at a leisurely pace as a form of modest exercise. The concrete sea wall along South Roosevelt runs past the airport along the Atlantic side of the island. There is a wide path for cyclists and joggers and if you time it right, a bikini or two headed for the beach. Okay, I said I was retired but I am not dead.

I hung around the seawall path to point out my find but really to get a break from the morning pedal in the already oppressive humidity. As usual I could count on at least ten minutes before a cop showed up. These are not priority calls in Key West.

As it happened, it was my former partner, Officer Jeff Sessions or *OJ* as we call him, who rolled up. And no, it is not for his Bronco driving skills, and no, he was not that kind of partner. Clarification is sometimes necessary in Key West as it is one of the more rainbow-oriented parts of the country.

After some pleasantries and catch up, OJ pulled an extension pole out of the cruiser trunk, snapped it open and began to hook, then drag the bundle to the beach by the wall. He seemed to be struggling and called for me to give him a hand.

"Don't just stand there," he shouted, "this thing must be waterlogged".

~ ~ ~

Attired in my typical flip-flops and shorts, I was more appropriately dressed to get wet so I dropped over the sea wall to push the bundle over the rocks and immediately knew something was very wrong.

"You need to call for back up dude. This is not your usual grouper. My bet is you are in for a long day."

The summer heat index began to rise even higher as the morning moved closer to noon. After what seemed like an eternity standing on the sea wall, two Key West detectives pulled up as well as the Medical Examiner to take charge of what turned out to be a torso in the bag. Finally they began loading it into the back of the ME's Chevy van. At that point, the detectives Davis and his partner Alice Martin decided that I should be grilled for whatever I might know.

For the next thirty minutes I was questioned.

"When did you first see the body? " to which I replied, "When the ME opened the wrapping."

Davis shot back, "Ok, smart ass, I know you were a cop but you're not any more so just answer the questions."

"When did you first notice the bundle?"

"About nine forty-five am."

"Where did you first notice the bundle?"

"When I rounded the turn going south past the East Martello Fort by the airport."

"Were you alone?"

"No there were other bikers and joggers on the path."

"Did you notice anything or anyone unusual in the area?"

"Yes, the square grouper in the water off the sea wall."

"Did you touch anything?"

"Yes, the bag after OJ asked me to help bring it ashore" etc., etc., etc. Being a smart ass is just in my DNA.

~ ~ ~

I was finally able to continue on my way and make it in time for my regular post-ride Bloody Mary at Southernmost Beach Café just as the clock struck eleven. Cindy, the bartender looked at me like "Where have you been Finn? I've been waiting since ten with a fresh batch of mix," to which I replied, "I am trying to pace myself. It's Sunday so I though I would catch the eight o'clock service then ride."

She smiled knowingly, "Right."

For the last three years, Cindy and I have had a running banter as I tried to seduce her and she tolerated my Peter Pan charms. Okay, some of you may be judging me for my morning drinking - more on that later. Some of you may question my taste in women – definitely more on THAT later.

Even though I was pretty thirsty, my Bloody Mary would have to wait a little longer. I grabbed my snorkel and mask out of the basket of my bike and headed across South Beach for my morning, or in this case, pre-lunch swim to the buoy and back for a half hour. I sound like a health nut but really I count calories and if I want the occasional cocktail, I need to burn a few during the day.

Refreshed and with a mild buzz after my now post swim Bloody Mary, I headed home to check emails, take a look at the markets in Japan, make my lunch salad and catch my retired guy Sunday power nap.

It's been three years since I left the force- read *was let go*; read was released to industry - read *got my ass fired.* That's a hard thing to have happen in Key West but my ex-wife claimed abuse. It was not true unless you consider that it crossed my mind more than once. It probably didn't help that she was the daughter of one of the 'Bubbas' - meaning influential families in the lower keys and that she was the original reason for my being on *The Rock* as locals call Key West.

Being a smart ass had not built up points with the brass and they seemed happy to get rid of me for any excuse. After eight years of marriage and eight years on the force I was footloose and fancy free. For the first six months I felt sorry for myself and spent most days at the Rum Bar drinking Bahama Bob's very excellent Dark and Stormys with a Bark Chaser. Seemed to fit both my mood and my attitude.

Finally after a particularly wicked weekend bender, Bob called my buddy and former Navy SEAL instructor in BUD/S, Matt Divine who came down from Miami, dragged me out of the bar and offered me a job handling insurance claims for his agency.

Before you think I am another Navy SEAL writing about the experience, I was a "BUD/S Dud" and rang out after my legs gave out humping *Old Misery,* a reported four hundred and fifty pound giant punishment log five months into BUD/S training. Being 6'3" is not the ideal size for a SEAL. Matt was a lifesaver after my *Drop on Request* or DOR and helped me realize it was not the end of the world. He seemed to show up whenever I was in trouble. Might have something to do with his last name.

Matt offered me a job investigating a weird claim involving a local Conch I'll call Smokey. There are three kinds of residents on The Rock: Salt Water Conchs who are born and raised on the island and sometimes called Bubbas; Fresh Water Conchs who have lived here more than seven years; and tourists.

Smokey was a pilot who took the seats out of his Cherokee 6, installed a mattress and used the plane for couples to join the mile high club. He was doing a bang up business flying fifteen hours a day off the southern coast of Key West until an elderly couple paid him a lot of cash to take them up.

Once airborne Smokey claimed they tried to hijack the plane to Cuba using a rusty penknife. After a fight in the cockpit - read pilot seat - the controls were damaged and he was forced to ditch the plane.

His two passengers opened their life jackets inside the plane and were not able to get out. They went down in it and Smokey was rescued. Without a paper trail the story was so farfetched it began to smell like insurance fraud and Matt was asked to investigate.

I took it on for want of anything more constructive to do and after a week looking into it including interviewing Smokey's two ex-girlfriends, always a source of venom, I concluded that Smokey had a very lucrative little gig going with *Smokey's Booty Airways*. However he was conducting a criminal enterprise with the aircraft thus voiding any insurance claim. Matt appreciated the help and I had found a use for my free time.

Now Key West is a tropical paradise and also the end of the road, literally the A1A, or Mile Marker 0. As a piece of local trivia, it is the most stolen mile marker in the Keys. It is also the end of the road for a varied collection of hucksters, hustlers, hookers and homeless.

Over the following year, I began to handle various investigations around the island from ex husbands hiding assets, to identity theft, missing persons and business fraud. My accounting degree - another long story - plus police experience, tended to give insurance companies a misplaced sense of confidence in my investigative abilities.

If you are curious, the misunderstanding leading to my being released to the job market, and 'the bitch leaving', as I called my wife divorcing me, is what led to the *woe is me six month binge.*

With Matt's help, I bought a fixer upper shotgun cottage on Catherine Street in Old Town and acquired Crutch my three-legged dog from the Key West SPCA shelter. I know, his name may seem a bit cruel but it seemed to make sense on several levels.

After my busy Sunday morning, I headed back to the house where Crutch lay cooling his three heels having his post morning constitutional nap. We headed out again after lunch walking along Duval and up South St. toward dog beach on a tour of his favorite trees and lampposts. He had a swim at the kelp-covered Dog Beach and I had a Stella at Louie's; it is Sunday after all.

As I considered another Stella and Crutch seemed content sniffing a cute little Australian Sheep dog, my cell phone rang and to my surprise the voice at the other end had an all too familiar ring, "Are you sober?' he said.

CHAPTER TWO

NOW YOU HAVE TO KNOW my ex father-in-law to appreciate his concern but he still pissed me off.

"What, I don't even get a hello after three years?"

'That was hello, asshole."

"Thanks for the call, Dad," and I hung up. He hates it when I call him Dad.

It is probably appropriate to share a little background at this point. Roger Linebush is the patriarch of one of the oldest dynasties in Key West. His family goes back to the early days of wrecking thus making him a true blue Conch.

Wrecking was the practice of retrieving cargo from ships that ran up on the reefs that surround Key West. It made Key West the richest city in the United States at one time.

I was married to his daughter for eight years until I put his son Wade in prison for fifteen. Wade was running a Ponzi scheme and had scammed investors out of over $15 million dollars. Needless to say I wasn't the Linebush family's favorite in-law nor his daughter's after that.

The phone rang again and I ignored it.

Wade was a trust fund kid with Daddy issues, ambition and a marginal intellect. He worked in his dad's construction company and after five years decided to branch out on his own. Using the family name and connections, he convinced several local families to invest in a land deal on Stock Island.

All seemed to be progressing well at first until after about two years, some off-island group bought the project. Wades company made a profit for himself and the investors so he raised money for a Marina project based on his track record.

The phone rang again and I answered.

"What." My idea of a pithy greeting.

"Ok, don't hang up."

" Why not?" Again my rapier wit.

"I need your help."

Now that stopped me in my tracks. Here is a scion of Key West society, the most successful developer in town, sometimes called the 'Darth Vader' of real estate developers and an accomplished entrepreneur. And he was asking for my help?

"Are you still there?" he asked.

"Yes ... . I was just checking with the devil to see if hell had frozen over. I seem to recall you saying it would be a cold day in hell before I would ever work again in this town."

"Who said anything about work?" he replied.

"So what you are asking for, a favor?" I laughed. This conversation was becoming surreal.

"Look Ernie, if you can put aside your ego for minute, I ..."

I hung up again.

I know you might think I should be more respectful, but calling me Ernie set me off. You see, my given name is Ernesto Finnegan Pilar. My father was Portuguese, my mother Irish. Dad was a huge fan of Ernest Hemingway, Mom of James Joyce. Hemingway's favorite fishing boat was the *Pilar*.

Destiny that I end up here, right?

My friends called me *Finn* in high school because of my middle name, my big feet and my state swimming records. The name stuck.

He called me back again.

"Look, Finn, just give me 5 minutes of your time. I would be very grateful."

"Let me get this straight, we haven't spoken in three years. I was the one who caught your son stealing from his investors, your daughter divorced me claiming abuse, you got me thrown off the force, and you are asking for a favor? Even for a Bubba, you got a lot of chutzpah."

"Finn, oddly enough all that is what makes you uniquely qualified for this and why I need you. I know we haven't always seen eye to eye but I have always respected your integrity."

I laughed and almost hung up but that felt repetitive and a bit petulant.

At this point, the more mature side of me was curious; Okay, the least immature side of me. I know what it must have taken for him to call and ask for help. Having him owe me one did have a certain appeal.

'When and where?" I asked.

Now this is not an idle question because Key West is a small town and most locals knew that I was persona non grata with the Linebush family. Me showing up at his office or at a local bar would be noticed.

"Drive over to Hurricane Hole and I will have a friend's boat pick you up, say four pm? Look for a Grady White named *Puppy Ciao.*"

I ordered another Stella and sat at the bar thinking about what Roger might need and about why I would even bother helping him. I concluded that I needed a therapist to sort out my issues around this family so I paid the full tab - no local discount at Louie's - collected Crutch from his amorous pursuit of the Aussie and we headed home. With a couple of hours to kill I figured a quick nap and a hot shower to wash off the salt after the swim were in order. About 3:45 we hopped on my scooter, Crutch perched comfortably on the floorboard between my legs. Driving on the island can be a pain and parking a nightmare. Scooters are the fastest, easiest way to get around if a bit high risk, but hey live dangerously, right?

We rode up Truman and onto North Roosevelt. Construction on the road was winding down after almost three years but traffic was heavy due to the last minute push to finish by the deadline. A lot was riding for Linebush Construction completing the job on time given the penalty clauses and they did not like to pay penalties.

~ ~ ~

Hurricane Hole is a low-key Stock Island marina one bridge off The Rock. It's a favorite with fisherman, service workers and hookers. Or so I have been told. The marina restaurant serves great Conch chowder and as we had a few minutes to kill, I ordered a bowl of the soup and a Dark and Stormy for me plus a Bud Light for Crutch.

With a full belly and a mild buzz from the Dark and Stormy, I looked out over the marina and spotted *Puppy Ciao* idling into the dock. One look at the skipper and I realized this could not be too top secret a mission. She was 5'10" with a bob of chestnut hair wearing a pink Green Parrot baseball cap and not much else. To call her stunning would be to call the Mona Lisa a nice sketch. It hardly begins to cover her impossibly long legs, tight firm ... well you get the idea. I always was an ass man.

Did I mention she was also my ex wife?

~ ~ ~

I first met Courtney in San Diego while I was working for a local CPA firm Murrill Gerbino doing my internship. She was a student at the University of San Diego doing her Masters in Real Estate. We met at Stingaree a club in the historic Gas Lamp Quarter. I was doing shots with a bunch of friends to celebrate my SEAL contract and she was getting ready for her finals. Studying was never her thing.

Puppy Ciao barely touched the dock and four burly fishermen were stumbling over each other offering to tie up her stern ... as well as the boat. It was hardly a discreet entrance as she grew up here and everyone knows her.

She still makes my heart skip a beat like a schoolboy crush on the head cheerleader but I was cool. I ambled down the dock with Crutch at my heel and the dregs of the Dark and Stormy in my hand. I had not seen her since the divorce three years ago but I had heard she was working in Miami in commercial real estate. Not that I kept track of course.

When I put her baby brother away for fraud, she lost it and tried to brain me with a boat hook. Aside from a bruised arm I was fine but restraining her caused bruising on her arms and she got a bump on her head when head butted me as I tried to calm her down. This morphed into assault and my eventual dismissal from the force for spousal abuse.

As much as I lusted after her today, the memory of that day kept my excitement to a minimum. Not that I didn't have a stirring or three.

Courtney seemed to have some of the same response, abject disgust mixed with animal lust but the latter could just be wishful thinking on my part. The bikini she chose to wear seemed to imply an interest but her scowl was a negative. Okay, I was a bit confused but this was not the first time I had received mixed signals from her.

She nodded for me to release the lines and jump aboard, as she fired up the engines. Now a Grady White is not a really fast boat but it is solid and dependable. The twin 300 Mercury Pros can move and Courtney has been ably handling boats since she was a teenager.

Once out of the no wake zone she hammered it and we were up on plane at thirty knots in a heartbeat. I am not sure if it was urgency or a desire to minimize conversation but the noise made conversation more difficult than it would have been anyway.

We were out to the backside of Wisteria, a small

twenty-two acre scrub island off the coast of Key West harbor in less than ten minutes.

We slowed as we came up on the motor yacht *Ciao Bella* anchored out about fifty yards from shore. Its dark blue hull and teak rails glistened in the afternoon sun. My ex-father-in-law sat on the deck with another man I had not seen before.

~ ~ ~

Roger Linebush is a small man, who dresses for the islands: linen shorts, pastel linen shirt, leather sandals and a panama hat. He is rarely without a cigar usually unlit but for affect. His guest was dressed in a similar fashion but with the cigar lit and the pants long.

You could cut the tension with a knife as Courtney brought the launch up to the back of the yacht. Stairs lead up both sides of the transom and a covered hot tub was just above the swim platform. *This was some boat.*

I followed Courtney up the stairs appreciating the view. The back end of the boat was nice as well.

As we came up on deck I realized why Roger looked nervous. The gun in the stranger's hand was a Colt Woodsman 22 with a silencer and it was pointed at Roger. Now this was a development.

The stranger was the first to speak. "Mr. Pilar, my name is Eduardo Ortega. Welcome to *Ciao Bella*. I hope that your stay will be pleasant."

I looked down at Crutch and said, "Thanks for the heads up, Lassie". Crutch hated it when I called him that.

Clearly I was expected to say something in response to the warm welcome so I offered, "Nice boat." I turned to Roger who was sitting quietly on the sofa and said, "I'm guessing your invitation has something to do with the gun pointed at your crotch. You want to fill me in?"

Roger responded in his usual genial fashion, "You really are an idiot aren't you Ernie?" a comment to which I would have turned and left but for the gun shifting towards me. I suppose he had a point, as I should have guessed that he would never have actually asked for my help unless he was under serious duress but I was out of practice and I missed it. The least I would have done was bring my own gun to the party.

"Well Roger, now that I am here what can I do for you after such a warm request?"

This is the point were Ortega spoke up and filled me in.

"Mr. Pilar, or should I call you Finn? Mr. Linebush and I have been having a nice chat this afternoon about the whereabouts of his Chief Financial Officer. It would seem that he has disappeared with a large sum of money much of which happens to be mine."

I am beginning to think his son's recent misfortune may have been the tip of the family iceberg.

"Look Ortega," Roger said, "I have been telling you all afternoon I am not aware of any money missing and Shawn Daniels is as honest as the day is long. He has been away for three days now on a family trip to Orlando to see the Harry Potter exhibit with his kids."

Ortega, looking skeptical said, "You Americans and your Disneyland."

"Disney World" I corrected him

"Whatever." He continued, "Mr. Linebush, I am delighted to invite you and your lovely daughter on a cruise aboard my vessel while your former son-in-law takes a few days to locate Mr. Daniels and bring him to me."

Turning to me, he spit out, "Mr. Pilar, you have seventy-two hours to find and deliver Mr. Daniels or I will begin sampling the pleasures of your lovely ex-wife as will my crew."

I laughed. "You must be kidding! These two have completely screwed up my life and now you expect me to help them. What were you thinking?" A smile crept onto Mr. Ortega's face. He leaned over and shot Roger.

CHAPTER THREE

ALL RIGHT, the shot only grazed his leg and ruined his shorts but it still must have hurt like a son of a bitch and it sure got my attention. Crutch leapt up and immediately ran down the stairs to the swim platform. I started to rethink my choice of breed. Maybe I should have looked at a Doberman or a German Shepherd.

The gun swung around to point toward me. Roger was yelling at me to take this guy seriously and Courtney sat whimpering on the deck. I have seen the damage a .22 can do in the right places and was not inclined to experience it first hand. So much for my indifference. Ortega tossed me the keys to the Grady White and repeated, "Seventy-two hours Finn, starting now."

As I fired up the engines of *Puppy Ciao*, I focused on the yacht. It was an impressive Feadship, about one hundred and eighty feet long with three decks and a twin jet Eurocopter on the stern of the middle deck. At about $7 million plus pilot, Mr. Ortega had more than a few million kicking around.

As I headed back to Garrison Bight I saw *Ciao Bella* weigh anchor and begin to steam toward the channel out of Key West.

So now what? I had no idea where to start and I am sure mine would not be a welcome face at Linebush Construction.

~ ~ ~

Like all good Gen Xers, I decided to Google the company to see what public information was available. I skipped my usual late happy hour at the Rum Bar much to Crutch's dismay. Bob the bartender is generous with the pretzel rods for him. He whined for two blocks as I drove passed the bar on the way home.

"Quit complaining," I told him. "You could stand to take off a pound or two and you need to watch your salt intake." I poured some Kibble in his bowl, threw a gourmet Stouffers Mac and Cheese in the micro and settled down at my computer.

A quick search revealed the CFO Shawn Daniels was forty-three years old, had been with Linebush for seven years after working at Ledcor in Canada and before that for Deloitte Consulting. He graduated from Northwestern with a Bachelor of Commerce. Blah, blah, blah. Nothing special so far.

A little deeper examination showed a guy making a six-figure salary that in Key West is not bad. His wife Sarah was on the board of the Key West Garden Club and Shawn was a contributing member to the Tropic Cinema. The kids, Emily twelve and David ten, went to Sigsbee Charter School. All in all, a typical fresh water conch in the upper middle tier of Key West life.

The company's website revealed several large projects in the works including a new hotel next to Schooner Wharf and a proposed marina expansion on Stock Island. I wonder if this is Wade's old Ponzi deal. These projects would require a lot of working capital. It might be worth looking at the ownership structures for both as a starting point.

I got the address for the Daniels' home on Washington Street and as the sun was going down I headed up Truman to White Street and down to Washington for a little drive by.

This area in Midtown is as you might imagine, a quiet street, a mix of large traditional Victorian style homes and new contemporary gated tropical style ranch homes set back from the street behind gates with lots of privacy palms, bougainvillea and coral block walls. The Daniels' place was no different and based on the lights at this point it appeared unoccupied. The only odd thing was three days of the Key West Citizen in a bush next to the circular driveway. Their drivers never can seem to get the daily paper over gates but they are usually good about not delivering if you go on vacation assuming you put in a request.

Crutch needed his early evening relief so we hopped off the scooter and took a stroll around the neighborhood. Few people suspect a man and his dog, even a three-legged one, doing evening rounds as being an investigator. Crutch did a masterful job of watering every tree on the block and naturally we ran into a neighbor with her dog.

"I saw you snooping over at the Daniels' place," she shared.

So much for my theory of a man and his three legged dog.

"Shawn asked me to check on the place," I replied. "I hadn't heard from him in a few days and thought I would come by." A quick recovery I thought.

"I saw him, the wife and the kids head out about three days ago which I thought was odd that they miss a day of school with finals around the corner. Seemed in a hurry as well."

Thank God for nosy neighbors.

I thanked her and said nice things about her little white dog like you are supposed to do, even though I regard them as more of a light snack than a real dog.

So what have I got?

Kids out of school and no paper cancellation. Not exactly Sherlock Holmes deduction at this point. It was time to give some further thought to this puzzle. We headed over to Schooner Wharf Bar to check out the newly built hotel and sample the rum.

As I pulled up and parked the scooter, Crutch headed for the bar. They keep a dog bowl under a stool. He likes a quick drink and to hang with his buddies. Doug, my morning hangover buddy was there with his two Huskies, Boca and Koda, and OJ was there with his Golden, Harley.

It was like a regular meeting of the Tuesday night poker club on an off night. After greetings and a six-inch Robusto from Miguel, we chatted a bit about life on The Rock.

I asked if any of them had noticed the big blue Feadship off Wisteria today and OJ shared that it belonged to a big time investor from Nicaragua named Ortega. The coast guard kept an eye on the ship as he was also a suspected drug dealer but they could never prove it. Great I thought, guns, money and now drugs.

I decided to make it an early night given the deadline I was fighting and headed home for few hours rest before my upcoming early morning research.

~ ~ ~

Key West is a party town and some bars along Lower Duval stay open until four am. College kids and wedding parties are usually carousing till the wee hours, and so are the cops. This makes it a bit more difficult to sneak around. Fortunately, Washington Street is more of a suburb and after three am is pretty quiet. Crutch stayed home. Actually he refused to get up at that hour, so I walked up United and across to Washington off White Street. It took about thirty minutes to case the joint; I love that Phillip Marlowe language.

I hopped the fence and tried the back doors. As usual the patio door was the weak point on these houses. I learned that as a cop from the B & E guys on the island. You can often just lift up on the slider and they pop out. It looks like Daniels did not take the precaution of putting a stop-lock or dowel across the bottom so I was inside in thirty seconds. It seemed I was not the first.

~ ~ ~

The place had been trashed. Furniture overturned and cushions cut open. Drawers were pulled out and garbage scattered. Either someone was rushing to get out and couldn't find the car keys or someone was ahead of me in the search for Daniels. *So what were they looking for ... ?*

A second floor bedroom was ripped apart as well but the light on the answering machine was flashing so I picked it up and listened.

"Hey asshole, if you think you can hide, forget it. You are dead and so is your family. We will hunt you down and make you regret the day you were born. See you soon."

It seemed the message was pretty clear. Daniels had made some nasty friends who were on his trail and ahead of me. It had been an unproductive evening but now I knew I wasn't the only one looking for Daniels.

As I came home, Crutch, rolled over, wagged his tail, farted and went back to sleep. What do I expect at five am? And it was too early for breakfast.

I was too wired to go back to sleep and it was too early to get much done so I took the lid off the Circle K coffee I picked up on the way home and opened yesterday's Key West Citizen. The lead story was about a 'square grouper' found by a concerned citizen. That would be me. Frankly a bit of an exaggeration I thought. It turned out to be the torso of a white male, dismembered, and decapitated. Gross. The story was asking for the public's help to identify the corpse. Well good luck with that.

I called OJ, knowing he would be awake and at the gym.

"What is it Finn? I'm working out."

"I know OJ, that's why I called. You always take longer rests between sets than anyone I know."

"Screw you," and he hung up. I called back and he was

more civil.

"Will you let me finish and call you back?"

"Sure, meet me at the Denny's in thirty minutes. You're buying." And I hung up.

Forty-five minutes later he strolled in, dressed in uniform and late just to be difficult. He sat down. "So what's up, that couldn't wait till office hours, Finn?"

"And good morning to you too," I quipped. "How was the work out?"

"Screw you, what do you need?"

"Isn't the pleasure of your company enough?"

"You don't call at five thirty in the morning for my company. What do you want?"

"Ok, I wanted to find out if you had any luck identifying the first body that showed up in the Salt Ponds by the airport last week."

Debra, my favorite waitress came by with coffee for OJ, a refill for me and we ordered: a Breakfast Burrito for him and the Grand Slam for me. While we waited for the food, he told me that it was a white male, early 40's with signs of living rough for some time. The cause of death was blunt force trauma to the head.

"He was in the mangroves for at least a week by the look of him and was pretty chewed up."

"Anything to identify him, prints, wallet, teeth, tattoos?"

"We have no ID but he has magnesium powder burns on his back in two arcs. These are fresh and on his back, where *Mara Salvatrucha* the drug gang that is heavily populated by Salvadorans, tattoo their members. The prints were burned off as well so we are sending his dental pictures to the FBI for their help."

I did my best not to flinch when he mentioned Mara given that Ortega was from that part of the world. Maybe Ortega was from Columbia not Nicaragua I mused.

"How about any connection with the Square Grouper I found?"

Our food arrived and I started eating as OJ talked.

"Now that is interesting," he continued. "So far we have some of the same magnesium powder burns on his back and shoulders which may show that he has burned-off tattoos but we can't be sure. He is heavily muscled and his chest showed signs of ink from a ballpoint pen that is usually used in Russian prison tattoos. He could have been an enforcer for one of the eastern European gangs."

"So what's next?" I asked but he was chewing a mouthful of burrito and ignored me. Debra brought the check with our local's discount and I pushed it over to him to pay. He laughed and pushed it back.

"I have to run Finn and don't you dine and dash. We know where you live," he chuckled as he strolled out. "I'll get you pictures," he said as he turned to head out the door.

Despite being stuck with the tab, I left Debra a generous tip on the table, paid at the cash register and at least I walked out a little better informed than when I started.

What do an eastern European muscle head with tattoos and a headless Salvadoran Mara Salvatrucha member have in common besides being dead in Key West? What do missing money, and a missing accountant have in common and could there be a connection to the two deaths?

CHAPTER FOUR

I NEEDED ONE of Cindy's Bloody Marys but Southernmost Café is not open until 8 am. I decided to grab Crutch and head over to Island Fit for a workout to clear my head.

The gym I use is on Truman and it's owned by my old friends Robyn and her husband Will Locke. They had their own troubles a few years ago when she was kidnapped in Key West from her wedding reception at South Beach. For a while Will was the main suspect; the husband is usually the first place to look.

I was working the case and it turned out that the man she thought was her long lost father was actually her real father's former partner (not that kind of partner). The father had died and the partner was trying to launder money by establishing fitness clubs around the country. That is a whole other story.

As I was going through my routine, it occurred to me that the muscle head would want to work out regularly and would probably use a local gym. I asked Robyn if she had any customers with either burns or heavy tattoos who was not showing up lately. While she didn't, I thought it might be a productive place to start.

After a quick shower and a power shake I started my day. There are only four decent gyms on the island so after about two hours I had been able to visit each of them. My last stop at Key West Island Gym on White Street hit pay dirt of sorts.

The girl behind the front counter remembered a guy who came in every day starting about a month ago but stopped coming last week. He had a heavy accent and what she called gang tattoos on his arms and shoulders. He pumped iron for a couple hours and left.

She remembered his name was Alexei something and he paid cash each visit rather than buying a membership. It was a start. I figured with some pictures of the tattoos she could ID him so I called OJ and left a message asking for any pictures he has of the Square Grouper body. I then headed for Southernmost Café and my daily ogle at Cindy and a Bloody Mary before my swim.

~ ~ ~

Cindy was waiting for me with the Bloody in the works as I walked in. Her Bloody Mary includes an in-house mix made with horseradish, a rim of Montreal Steak seasoning and Celery Salt and topped off with three blue cheese olives and a dill pickle. *True perfection.*

Just as I was settling in for my fifteen-minute morning banter, an out-of-place skinny Cubano looking guy in a loose fitting white linen suit strode into the bar adorned with a lot of gold chains, Cuban heels and attitude. Now you need to understand that in Key West the only guys who wear suits are either grooms or defendants. He looked like neither, though on reflection, he had that pasty look that often means prison or residents in Buffalo in January so a defendant was not out of the question.

With him was a knuckle dragger who looked like a bodyguard: tight shirt, pumped up biceps, and a gold chain. A poster boy for a indiscrete security detail.

The defendant looked around the bar settling his gaze on me and came charging over toward my stool. I keep my cool as he came within range, grabbed my wrist with his left hand and tried to spin me around off my stool.

"Hey asshole, who the fuck do you think you are, fucking my wife?"

Now this is one of those questions that is a bit like "When did you stop beating your wife?" If I ask "Who is your wife?" it can mean I am sleeping with so many I will need to know more information or that she was not memorable. Alternately, I am trying to buy time to think up some excuse for sleeping with someone's wife not knowing if she's his or not. Neither does much to diffuse the situation.

I chose to reach around, remove his hand from my arm with a wristlock moving to his left, standing up with his wrist trapped by my left twisting him to his knees. The bodyguard was about to step in so using the defendant's arm I used an elbow spiral to steer him to the ground between us.

Did I mention that I had be an Aikido student for the past three years as part of my health and fitness program?

"Tell your gorilla here to back off or you're going to need a cast for your wrist," I suggested to my new dance partner who immediately squeaked, "Leslie, it's okay," after which Leslie backed off. It was all I could do to not laugh. It is no wonder Leslie was a steroid junkie. With a name like Leslie he had to have taken a lot of grief in his neighborhood.

I released the defendant asking, "Now what do you want that it is so important you have to interrupt my morning BM?"

"You went off yesterday in a boat out of Hurricane Hole and my wife was driving. I know you were married to her and you got divorced so the only reason you could have gone off with her was if you are fucking her on the side."

Now to say I was *gobsmacked* was an understatement on so many levels. Courtney was remarried? To this asshole? And he thought I was fucking her? Wow.

My only response was, "You are out of your fucking mind," to which he seemed to forget the wristlock I used on him and decided to take a swing at me. I stepped in to it, blocked with both hands, grabbed his wrist and reversed it to lift his elbow above his head while holding his wrist and dropped him again to the ground.

Leslie stepped in with a hard right that I blocked with a Kotegaeshi. I took his wrist, drove his elbow into his stomach and feeling his wrist snap, dropped him to the ground on top of the defendant. Cindy was watching this from behind the bar with a look of shock but both of them were out of the fight before it was even noticed in the restaurant next to the bar.

~ ~ ~

As I surveyed the damage, OJ was arriving to bring photos of the two bodies that had shown up in the last week. He walked in through the restaurant's main entrance. Before OJ spotted me, Leslie the gorilla boy and the defendant scurried - no, scrambled - out the back exit of the bar onto the beach and I sat back down on my stool with my Bloody Mary. OJ slid in beside me and asked why I had blood on my forehead. I guess I got clipped in the little altercation.

"Hit it on the bar bending down to pick up a twenty." I improvised. No point in stirring things up at this point.

"So you're buying the next round?" he smiled.

"What are you having?" to which he frowned and said, "Still on duty dude, so I'll take a rain check."

Before I checked out the crime scene photos, I had to ask, "Did you know that Courtney had remarried?"

There was a long pause.

"Where did you hear that?" he avoided my question.

"You are not answering my question, OJ, did you?"

Two can play this game.

"Ok, I heard rumors that she had met some guy on a trip to Vegas and got married by one of those Elvis impersonator preachers but I didn't take it seriously."

"Well it appears you may not have taken it seriously

but it seems her new husband did. Just as you were coming in, he left with his goon bodyguard after trying to shake me down for supposedly having my way with her."

"What, you and Courtney are back together again!" OJ exclaimed.

"No, you idiot, but this Vegas dude seems to think we are and he was pissed about it."

"Finn, I have told you about keeping it in your pants."

"Look just forget it, ... here is why I called you."

Briefly I outlined my update and he agreed to go over to the gym and see if the girl at the counter recognized the Russian tattoos and see if anyone else at the gym recognized the victim.

~ ~ ~

We parted company, and after I finished my Bloody Mary, I headed into the ocean for my swim. The warm Atlantic water felt good on my stressed muscles and helped me release the adrenaline from my dust up with the 'defendant' and his gorilla.

As I swam between the buoys off South Beach and dodged the trains of jet skis racing by, I thought about what I had so far. Two bodies, assorted body parts, a missing accountant, a rich guy who has kidnapped my ex-wife and her father and a run in with the jilted husband of my ex and his pissed off body guard. Not bad for about 24 hours on a sleepy island. What's next I wondered?

~ ~ ~

I spent the afternoon with Crutch, trying to track down my ex's new husband. An internet search of marriage licenses in the last two years in Vegas was a bust. There are over seventy-five hotels and Bed and Breakfasts in Key West not to mention vacation rentals and having seen this pair, several trailer parks were in the running as well.

A break came when I got a call from my broker Eddie

Ransom asking about my call positions for next month. With a name like that, some days it feels like he holds my assets for 'ransom'. Over the past two years I had been making a decent living selling covered calls and naked puts.

These are a low risk way to earn income and buy stocks. I sell covered calls on stocks I own and collect a small premium with each call contract. I also sell puts on stocks I am interested in owning to get them at a bargain or collect the put premium. I have been earning about forty thousand dollars a year doing this so it keeps the wolf from the door.

Courtney started doing this when we were married and uses Eddie as well. I told Eddie I had run into Courtney's new husband at Southernmost Café. I said that he and I had chatted for a few minutes over drinks. Okay, it's sort of true as we did chat in addition to our scuffle.

I need to get his name so I said, "I wanted to send him my card but couldn't remember his last name."

Without thinking Eddie just replied, "So you met Peter?"

I thought he was a bit of a dick so the name fit.

"Yes, Peter. What is his address?" I was surprised when Eddie gave me his last name and an address on Sunset Key.

Sunset Key is a twenty-seven acre private island just off the coast of Key West Harbor. It is a very affluent community of about fifty homes and a Westin Hotel. I had never seen the guy in town and it is a small town so I was surprised and said so. Eddie said it belonged to his family and he is only there occasionally.

I asked Eddie to sell some thirty-day calls for me and gave him a list. He only charges me a flat fee so I have him handle it. We chatted a bit about the markets and signed off.

So Peter was a local with money. What is he doing with Courtney? How long have they known each other? Where is he when he is not here? Just more questions but at least a place to start.

CHAPTER FIVE

IN KEY WEST, the library on Fleming contains the historical records of the island including most property ownerships going back almost two hundred years. I decided to do a search and Tom, the head of the Historical section housed in the back room, helped me trace the ownership of Peter's house on Sunset Key.

The island itself was bought by a local developer in 1986 then resold in 1994. The house was built by Peter's family in 1987 for two million dollars, which back then would have been a significant price.

"Who is this guy?" I muttered and Tom overhearing me said, "So you don't know the name?" I mumbled something about being new in town and not knowing all the Bubbas in Key West yet to which he began his story about this old influential family on the island.

"The Cross family have been here for over one hundred and fifty years and started their fortune as wreckers. Originally part of a small group of Greek spongers, the Cross family, which is Stavros in Greek, came to the Bahamas but then as wrecking became lucrative moved to Key West in the 1860's. Wrecking was a major industry in the Keys from the 1820's to the early 1900's. At one point, Key West was the richest city in the country with a wreck almost every week being salvaged in and around the Lower Keys."

Tom searched around for some historical photos. "The Cross family had stayed in Key West developing a prosperous marina and yacht club on Stock Island. They were politically connected but not high profile and many family members had moved off the island to other parts of Florida."

Tom knows everything there is to know about this island. "Old man Cross, was a sly and crafty wrecker who had a fast skiff built so he could get to the wrecks first and lay claim before others got close. He also built a big house with a widow's walk on top so his crew could spot wrecks as early as possible. It was rumored that he put lights out on floats to indicate shoals that did not exist in order to drive ships onto unmarked reefs. It was never proven."

The ship and cargo would be taken into Key West for auction and half the value at auction went to the owner of the wrecking operation. Eventually old man Cross's son took over the business and the old man served as an arbitrator who often decided what percentage of a wreck would go to salvage."

"Sweet deal," I thought

"After the courts took over the arbitration process, the old man got himself elected as a judge and continued his 'most favored salvager' behavior. Wrecking eventually died off as navigation aids became more widely available and the family switched to land development, building hotels and homes as far north as Marathon. There was always a bit of a taint to their name and over the years they were suspected of involvement in classic Florida land scams and even drug running but nothing ever stuck."

I began to wonder what connections the Cross and the Linebush families had developed over the years and Tom again was very helpful.

"Those two families fought for years over wrecks, cigar manufacturing, land deals and even Key West bus tours. They made the Hatfields and McCoys look like Fred and Ginger."

When he saw my blank stare he said, "Laurel and Hardy?" Still nothing so he said, "Sonny and Cher?"

Ok, now I got it.

"So how is it that Peter and Courtney got married?"

It was his turn to stare.

"You're kidding right?"

"No, I found out this morning that they got married two years ago." I shared.

"Now that is weird." Tom said shaking his head.

~ ~ ~

Tom's help actually raised more questions than answers, but a wise friend of mine once said, *the problem you name is the problem you solve*, so my most important first step is to correctly name the problem.

This cast of characters was getting bigger by the hour. We have the Linebush family; father shot, son in jail, daughter my ex now married to a Cross. We have Cross's body guard Leslie, the deceased Alexi, and a no name body plus the missing accountant Daniels and his family with a mystery voice on their answering machine. Finally, we have the apparent yacht owner Ortega with a Colt Woodsman 22.

It was time for Crutch to have his constitutional and for me to have a swim to clear my head. As Crutch and I walked along Whitehead toward Front Street, I contemplated what it took to remain successful and wealthy for one hundred and fifty plus years on a small island like Key West. This place had consumed such men as the fabulously wealthy Henry Flagler, an early investor in Standard Oil who built the Overseas railroad to Key West in the early part of the 20th century only to have it destroyed in the Labor Day Hurricane of 1935.

His fantastic fortune, worth almost one billion dollars today was largely dissipated by his third wife's family in the 1960's.

How is it that the Linebushs and the Crosses continue to prosper today? Or do they? Where does the Cross money come from now? Where does Ortega fit in the puzzle? I think it is back to Google to see if I can learn more about him.

~ ~ ~

Back home I fired up my laptop and searched for the *M/Y Ciao Bella*. It turns out to be a Feadship built in 2009 for a South American agricultural baron, Eduardo Ortega.

Bingo! *I wondered what they meant by agricultural baron?*

The big blue-hulled boat is a one hundred and eighty foot long multi-deck behemoth with a range of 4,200 miles and sort of hard to miss in Key West.

The pictures of the boat online showed the deck where Roger was sitting when he was shot. Assuming the guy I met was actually Ortega, then at least I knew who was holding Courtney and Roger. The *where* and *why* were still unanswered questions.

A Google search of Ortega produced almost 3 million hits so that was of little help. Having said that, when tied to the name *Ciao Bella*, it produced an article from Yachting Magazine about the launch party for the boat.

The picture of the launch party was a bit blurred but it looked enough like the guy I met on the boat that it was safe to say it was Ortega. The shock came when standing in the background was Roger Linebush all smiles and holding a flute of champagne. What the fuck?

It seems that Ortega grew up in the streets of Managua and made his fortune first cleaning the basements of houses in new residential developments, eventually building homes, then developing commercial property. He bought farmland and began building a ranch. Now Ortega turns out to be a suspected cartel member using his farms in the Pacific lowlands to produce cocaine and smuggling it in to the US.

Great, this is getting more confusing. I have a dead Russian mob enforcer, a Nicaraguan cartel member who kidnapped my ex-wife and her father and a missing accountant and his family. I know what your thinking, some guys might celebrate their ex's getting kidnapped by drug lords.

Well maybe a little part of me enjoyed the irony of me being considered the bad guy in our marriage, her being kidnapped and them coming to me for help. Reality is that I still cared for Courtney and would do everything I could to get her back; maybe not so much for Roger.

A lot of blanks still needed to be filled in.

Crutch was whining at the door and I realized I had not eaten since last night so I thought I would head over to Garbo's Grill for a couple of fish taco's. Garbo's is a food truck on Caroline Street run by a friend and former handyman turned chef, Elvis and his wife. I phoned ahead so I could avoid the usual long line and headed over to pick them up.

~ ~ ~

Sitting on the beach at the end of Simonton watching the Fury boats sail past and munching on a couple of Mahi tacos with a cold Stella from Lagerheads Beach Bar is about as good as it gets. I could almost forget that my ex and her father were being held hostage by a suspected drug dealer. What was Roger doing with Ortega and why did he owe him money? From my days as a cop I learned that if you follow the money, you usually find the motive. So I decided to visit Eddie Ransom to see if he could shed some light on the situation with Linebush Co.

I had originally met Eddie several years ago through Courtney. After waiting a few minutes in his office, he returned from a client meeting and we sat down to chat. He seemed oddly distracted so I asked him how his day was going.

"It has been a little crazy today." He sighed running his hand through his thinning hair.

"I have a client looking to dump his portfolio in

anticipation of a market meltdown and I spent the last hour showing him what the tax consequences would be to dump it. In the end he said dump half so I have only an hour or so to get it done. What do you need?"

"I just have a quick question that you might be able to help me with."

"Ok, shoot." he said as he began scanning his computer screen for trading information.

"I have a client who has asked me to look into the financial health of Linebush Construction and I have not been able to get a hold of either Roger or his accountant. It could mean a big project for Linebush Construction and I am stuck. Where would you look to find the information?"

Ok, I am not being entirely truthful here but Ortega is sort of a client and I guess saving the lives of Courtney and Roger is sort of a big deal, at least to them.

Eddie paused and thought about it for a minute. "Finn, I have access to his portfolio as you know but I am not able to share with you anything about it."

"I know" I replied, "but if you could point me in the right direction that would help."

After a longer pause Eddie seemed to hesitate then said, "Finn, the Linebush family is the oldest client I have and were the first to invest with me when I came down here twenty years ago. You and I have known each other for seven or eight years but I just can't help you with this, I'm sorry."

Before I could even respond, he said dismissively, "Finn, I need to get back to work for the client I mentioned and I need to place a bunch of sell orders before the market closes so if you will excuse me ... " With that he turned back to his computer and began to type.

While I was a bit put off, I said I understood and left, Crutch trailing behind me. That was weird. Eddie has been a good friend for a long time and has never blown me off in the past. WTF? Was there a problem with the Linebush Construction accounts and if there was, where do I go from here? As I walked up Greene Street toward Schooner Wharf I paused and looked back at Eddie's office in time to see him headed down Simonton toward Caroline. He had just told me he had all these trades that needed to be done right away. Where was he headed in such a rush?

CHAPTER SIX

"OKAY," I SAID TO CRUTCH. "Let's do a little sneaky detective stuff," and off we went. I caught a glimpse of him as he turned up Caroline toward the Steam Plant Condominiums and followed at about fifty feet. He stopped at West Marine, then after about five minutes came out and continued on to the Steam Plant building. I waited about ten minutes and I saw him come out of the building with the 'defendant' from Southbeach Café, Peter Cross. They headed to the marina next to Schooner Wharf.

This is getting very strange. Old Man Cross and Roger Linebush supposedly despise each other and Peter Cross is married to Courtney. What is Eddie doing with Peter and where are they headed? None of this was making any sense.

Peter and Eddie walked on to the Boathouse and sat down for Happy Hour. Rather than watch them simply talk together I decided it was time to call on one of my long time sources, Colonel Dave.

Dave is a retired Full Bird Colonel in the Rangers who after moving to Key West twelve years ago has become something of an expert on the comings and goings on The Rock. He can usually be found at the White Tarpon around this time so I headed in that direction. He was seated at the bar with his usual Dark and Stormy, chatting with a long time Conch named DJ who owned a local Laundromat.

I sat down at the bar and ordered a round for them both. DJ passed saying he needed to get back to solve some clogged drain issues. Dave thanked me for the drink and we chatted for a bit about several mutual friends.

After the niceties, I asked Dave if he knew anything about the Linebush family. He laughed and asked me if it wasn't a little late for that given that I was a member of the family for eight years.

I admitted that he was probably right but I was actually looking for more of a historical perspective. He talked a bit about the world of wrecking and the cigar business, all of which I knew about, so I asked, "What about any rumors, local gossip, old wives tales, etc.?"

Dave paused and thought for a moment or two and began his tale. "Many local Conchs have wondered how it is that the Linebush family have stayed so rich through all the ups and downs over the last hundred and fifty years. One rumor that has persisted is the 'Linebush treasure'.

That one stopped me in mid drink. "The what?"

"Look I am not saying it's fact but the story is the Linebush patriarch Enoch Linebush was working on a rumored wreck off shore in sixty feet of water in 1885. Do you know the story behind the *Atocha*?"

I had of course, heard the story and even visited the Mel Fisher Maritime Museum in Key West a few times but wanted to hear Dave's point of view.

"What are you saying?"

Dave resumed his narrative. "The story of the *Atocha* starts with the departure of a fleet of twenty-eight Spanish galleons traveling from Havana back to Spain in 1622. Several of the ships were carrying cargo with values beyond imagination. The *Atocha* alone was carrying forty tons of silver and gold and seventy pounds of emeralds."

I couldn't even get my arms around those numbers.

"The *Atocha* with her crew of two hundred and sixty-five was hit by a severe hurricane on September 6th, 1622, just as she entered the Florida Straits. The ship sank with all of her treasure and crew off the coast of Key West. The Spanish dispatched five ships to salvage the Atocha once news of the disaster found its way back to Havana, but the treasure could not be recovered."

Boy, did he ever know his history.

"The rumor is that Enoch Linebush found a portion of the *Atocha* treasure over a hundred years before Mel Fisher found his portion which was thought to be worth about $450 million dollars. What Fisher found was only half of the total treasure. Enoch, rather than declare it and then try to deal with half the other wreckers in Key West, decided to simply 'farm' it occasionally bringing up coins and gems and selling it as wreckers spoils and old family jewelry."

Somehow, this didn't seem as crazy as it sounded.

"They have used it to support the family and did not go public with the find in order to avoid state taxes and payments to Spain. They kept it as a family secret with only the eldest child being aware of its location."

I sat stunned in my chair trying to fathom - pun intended - how a family could keep a secret for a hundred years but at the same time I didn't dismiss it out of hand either.

Assuming it was true, what would it mean for this case? The Linebush family is already rich from their construction company so this doesn't change anything. I can't see this impacting the situation; none of it made any sense.

I thanked Dave, bought him another drink and decided to head home. I needed to organize my thoughts. Crutch fell in beside me and we walked along Simonton in the shade of the buildings and majestic old trees, lost in thought.

~ ~ ~

The car that clipped me as I stepped off the curb was running the light on Fleming. Crutch barked at the last second and I looked up in time to avoid a full step into the street. I spun around and bounced off the driver's side window onto the sidewalk next to the China Garden restaurant. By the time I focused, the car was gone and I had only a vague impression of the driver as white and wearing a grimy green Harley Davidson cap.

Several people stopped and asked if I was okay. Someone called 911 and I sat on the ground in shock supporting my sore ribs and my ankle throbbing uncontrollably. The ambulance service from up on North Roosevelt pulled up a few minutes later. You can hear them coming for a good five minutes as they love to run with the sirens on full blast. It is supposed to make the victim feel better knowing that help is on the way. It really just irritates everyone along the route. I was trying to stand up without much success.

It turned out the EMT was an old friend Steve Roberts from my cop days with his partner Jim Foley. And yes that kind of partner. Steve is an import like many on The Rock, in his case from Ireland.

Steve came over and said, "Tis a bit early in the day, to be fallin' down, isn't it Finn?"

To which I replied in my best Irish brogue, "You can-nee drink all day if you don-nee start in the marnin, Steve."

He laughed and said. "Pathetic effart, dear boy. Now what happened te ye?" he asked.

Not wanting to make a big deal about it I said, "Just some drunk tourist decided to try and catch the light and clipped me as I stepped off the curb. He kept on going and may not have even known he hit me. Crutch here barked at the last second and saved me arse. He just wanted to make sure I feed him tonight." I managed a weak smile.

Jim began checking the ankle and when he touched it I couldn't help but wince. It was already beginning to swell and they lifted me up to see if I could walk on it. It was not fun but I put some weight on it and while painful, I still could walk.

"I don't think it's broken but you should get it x-rayed," Jim suggested. "Take it easy, elevate it and ice it for the next couple of days then decide if you want to get it looked at."

Yeah, take it easy, right I thought.

Given that there was no blood, bone through skin or serious injuries, the gawkers drifted away and Jim offered to give me a lift back to my place.

As Steve and I sat in the back of the wagon, he turned and asked me, "So what really happened, Finn? You obviously spun around, bounced off the car after you got hit. Your t-shirt is ripped and your ribs are bruised from hitting the driver's mirror. Don't bullshit me."

Did I mention that Steve was smart? "I honestly don't have a clue," I said. "I didn't see him for more that a split second and he had a cap on with sun glasses. The truck was dark colored but that is it."

"So are you working on a case that might cause an ex-husband to want you dead?" Steve joked. "You know you don't always make friends in your line of work."

"Steve, I am offended. Everybody I know loves me. I am just a simple guy who occasionally helps some poor lonely woman get what she is entitled to from her cheating husband."

He laughed, "Yeah right, so who is your vic this week?"

"You know I cannot discuss my clients but he is a fine upstanding local judge caught playing 'hide the sausage' with a bailiff much to his wife's dismay. She asked me to look into it."

Steve replied, "Your client is a bitch and we all know who you are talking about. He shows up at La Te Da for the tea dance about once a month so he's already out."

This was just a shot in the dark on my part as the

judge was the one who granted Courtney our divorce. Starting a rumor was my little way of taking my revenge.

"Don't say anything Steve, I appreciate it." I knew it would be all around town by this evening and he wouldn't be talking about me.

We arrived at my cottage and Crutch and I hobbled up the steps like a couple of drunken twins and I headed for the freezer. I took out the vodka, poured a stiff shot, lay down and held the bottle against my ankle. Steve said to ice it so I was just following medical advice.

~ ~ ~

I woke up with a start and realized I had dozed off. The sun was coming up and I had lost the full night. The vodka was untouched and the ankle was painful as hell. Thinking better of the shot first thing in the morning, I went into the bathroom and dug out some old Vicodin I had left over after a beating I got from a couple of fishing buddies. I had tried to arrest them as they were trying to dump *square guppies,* one-ounce packs of cocaine, over the side of their boat to avoid being caught. This kind of small time stuff is common with college kids down for spring break.

Yes, I could see that the Vicodin was over three years old but that makes it aged like cheese right? I popped a couple and dry swallowed them, then moved over to my computer. I may have been a little less than candid with Steve and Jim in describing the vehicle that hit me.

As I was falling down I was up close and personal with the rear bumper and I recognized the bumper sticker. It was an annual pass for the Stock Island Marina. The one that was involved in the fraud scheme run by Courtney's brother. It was a thin lead but I might be able to track it down.

A quick Google search confirmed the logo on the parking pass so against my better judgment, given my banged up ribs, I fed and watered Crutch, then hobbled up to Bad Boy Burrito for a Burrito-to-go at the Bottle Cap Bar on Catherine. Back at the house, I gingerly loaded Crutch on the floorboard of the scooter and headed to Stock Island.

CHAPTER SEVEN

STOCK ISLAND MARINA VILLAGE was a newer facility just beginning to look a little worn from three years of ocean salt, jet fuel from the Boca Chica military base and marginal maintenance. The two hundred slips were only about half full and the shops were just making rent. Today it was being turned around by a group of the investors.

Five years ago, Courtney's brother had pitched it to investors as a draw for big yachts, a future hub for wealthy owners to anchor in the southernmost point in the U.S.A. No one said Wade was a poor salesman. He did run into a problem when he sold the shares promising returns of twenty percent a year.

When the slips did not sell, he continued to sell shares using the money to provide the early investors with the twenty percent telling himself that once the slips sold he would make up the difference. After two years, new investors dried up and returns disappeared.

I began an investigation after a family dinner I attended with Courtney blew up when the old man would not bail Wade out. It turned out that he had sold a hundred and fifty percent of the company. That is most people's definition of a Ponzi scheme and stock fraud. Wade was convicted in part based on my testimony about the dinner and sentenced to eight years in prison.

The rest of the family was able to avoid prison again based on my testimony but that didn't prevent them from kicking me out of future family dinners, not to mention, birthdays, Thanksgiving and Christmas. The divorce followed and eventually my dismissal from the force.

Going back to the marina brought back all the

previous memories of the whole thing as I rode through the stone gates. A group of the original investors had taken it over and turned it into a functioning, if not yet thriving, operation.

I headed to the office and the girl behind the desk looked vaguely familiar. It turned out she was Stacy Barnett, the daughter of one of investors who took over control of the marina after Wade went to jail. When I last saw her almost four years ago, she was only a kid working summers after her junior year in college.

To say she had grown up was an understatement. In her cut offs and midriff cut tee shirt, it was clear that nature had blessed her with all her bits and pieces well designed. After I caught my breath I put on my most winning smile and mumbled eloquently, "Stacy, it has been a long time."

To my surprise she smiled back and said, "Finn, it is nice to see you again."

Smooth as always I asked, "When did you get back to The Rock? It must be, what, four years?"

She paused. "Almost. I left to go back to college and law school after Dad took over the Marina from that crook Wade. Sorry I know he's your brother-in-law but he really screwed over a lot of people including my Dad."

I shook my head and corrected her. "My *ex* brother-in-law, Courtney and I got divorced after the trial."

Oddly, Stacy smiled. "Really? Dad didn't mention that, but then why would he?"

We both paused, and my thought bubble was *be careful idiot, she can't be more than 25 and you are pushing 40.*

I could only calmly say, "Well, welcome back."

"Thanks, so now that I know you didn't come in to see just me, how can I help you?" My next thought bubble was …. You can use your imagination.

46

My actual response was, "I was near Fausto's this morning and a blue pickup clipped a tourist on a bike coming out of the lot. I ran over to the cyclist to see if he was okay and when I looked up the truck was turning the corner. All I could see was a sticker on the bumper that looked like a marina sticker.

There was also one of those bumper stickers that reads JESUS LOVES YOU, EVERYONE ELSE THINKS YOU'RE AN ASSHOLE. I thought I would come up here and see if I could find it or maybe who owns it."

Stacy thought for a second and said, "Let me look at our records before I confirm for sure but it sounds like Squeaky MacKay, a mechanic for Linebush Marine. He was let go a couple of months ago for drinking on the job."

I asked her to check and see if she had an address and while she looked on the computer I thought, "Wow, if he was driving, this was getting very complicated."

I had busted Squeaky several times back in the day for DUIs mostly but also for stealing engine parts from boats moored long term in the harbor. Owners would leave their boats for weeks at a time. He would keep an eye on them, then slip aboard and steal parts. I put him away for two years on his second offense and he didn't seem to appreciate his *three hots and cot* from the state.

A minute later Stacy handed me a note with an address for Squeaky. Attached to it was a card with her name and the name of a law firm.

Not being able to think of a way to stick around and feel like a dirty old man, I thanked her and went back out to my scooter. Crutch was on guard duty and looked up from his nap, yawned, stretched and climbed on the bike.

As I got on the scooter I noticed Stacy looking out the office window and I waved. She smiled and waved back as I rode out the gates.

~ ~ ~

Riding down Shrimp Road, I decided a quick bite of early lunch at Hogfish Bar & Grill was in order and it is Crutch's favorite restaurant. Hogfish is a local delicacy that many on the island prefer to almost any catch. It is a light firm fish that is served with a citrus beurre blanc sauce on a soft roll. It would bring tears to the eyes of a marble Madonna. But I digress.

Hogfish is right on the water where the fishing boats come to off load so Hogfish gets their fish *first off the boat*. Between the fish sandwich, spicy Bahamian conch chowder and a cold Bud Light, it is an island paradise.

As I waited for the food, I took out the note from Stacy to look up the address and noticed that not only was she an attorney but on the back of the card was her name, a phone number and the word *Dinner?* Now that was a pleasant thought.

I know some of you might think that a handsome, well-educated and buff player such as myself would be busy almost every night. Since my divorce I had not been with anyone, as much as my carefully cultivated reputation might suggest otherwise. When things settled down, I would definitely follow up with Stacy.

With Crutch sitting between my legs on the floorboards of the scooter, I decided to cruise by the trailer park on Northside Drive near Kennedy. It's a collection of aging trailers with low rents and known locally as *workforce housing*. It is the type of place that Squeaky might call home. That or a bar stool at Schooners.

As the sun was beginning its slow Caribbean descent off high noon toward the horizon, I parked the scooter and with Crutch on a leash we walked through the entrance to the park. The address Stacy gave me was about a third of the way into the park on my left. As we walked up the crumbling cement walk, I ran through my head what I would ask him.

"Why did you try to run me down?" was not likely to solicit a candid reply and "Up against the wall asshole", while an attractive option, was not likely to produce much either. In the end I just walked up to the corroded screen door and knocked.

A tired looking middle-aged women in a faded cotton dress came to the door and without prompting said, "He's not here and no I don't know when he'll be back." Something told me this was not the first time someone had been at her door looking for Squeaky.

I thought of trying the old *Publishers Clearing House Sweepstakes* trick but decided I couldn't keep a straight face so I just asked, "When did you last see him?"

She offered it was yesterday afternoon when he left for work. I said it was important I speak with him and asked where he worked. After a pause, she said, "the asshole owes me money, so if you find him tell him the rent is due. If he's not at the Cross engine repair shop at Garrison Bight, then you'll find him at the VFW on North Roosevelt. Tell him from me if he doesn't pay the rent then we are done."

Clearly this was another case of marital bliss in the Keys. I would be at the VFW too if this was my life on the home front. Crutch was back on the scooter and ready to go before I had my scooter key out. Clearly he didn't like the neighborhood any more than I did.

~ ~ ~

The VFW was a little more than staggering distance away so after consulting with Crutch we headed over. Walking into the VFW was a blast from the past. A bunch of military dudes huddled over bourbon and beer reminiscing about buddies lost and battles fought in wars from Asia to the Afghanistan.

As my eyes adjusted to the dim lighting and my body to the chilled air, I wandered over to the bar, showed my

Navy ID and ordered a Bud Light. I had a long night ahead.

George the bartender remembered me from my binge days and asked how I had been. I lied and said things were great and we swapped lies for a few minutes about mutual friends in far away lands. Most of my buddies can't talk about where they have been and where they are now, so we all lie.

I eventually asked George if he had seen Squeaky and after a brief pause he said, "that asshole hasn't been in here since he got in a brawl with a couple of guys from Miami a couple of days ago. They beat him pretty good and he took off in his truck without paying his tab. Seems he owed them money as well for some gambling debt. If you find him drag his ass in here so we can settle up."

I thanked George for his help and paid for my beer. Now what? I slipped to the back of the bar and on a napkin tried to sort out what I had so far.

I know that Courtney and Roger are being held by Ortega off shore on his boat, and I suspect Ortega is a drug dealer. I suspect Roger either needs money or owes money to Ortega. I know that Courtney is married to Peter *The Defendant* Cross. I know that Shawn Daniels the accountant is missing perhaps with his family.

I know we have two dead bodies and suspect at least one is a Russian mobster and the other may be a Nicaraguan gang member. I know that Eddie Ransom works with both Courtney and I and he was acting strange when I went to see him. I know Eddie met with Peter Cross after I asked him a bunch of questions about Peter.

I know that Squeaky MacKay used to work for Linebush Marine and now works for Cross. This is a small town. I suspect he may have been driving the truck that tried to run me down shortly after I met with Eddie.

It was time to go old school: motive, opportunity and means.

CHAPTER EIGHT

THE MAJOR MOTIVES for murder fall into four categories: love, lust, lucre and loathing or some combination of all four. The sub-categories that seemed to support the evidence so far include:

Keeping a secret (Lucre, or Love); Money (Lucre); Urge to protect (Love); Revenge (Loathing); and Drugs (Lucre).

I did not see *Urge to protect (Love)* in my mix yet but all the others seemed possible.

Ortega was trying to collect money by finding the CFO, as was the voice on Daniels' voicemail. Someone had killed one or more people. Are they related to this case or not? Linebush may have a secret stash of treasure that he wants to keep secret. Ortega may be a drug dealer or just a rich farmer.

I figured that I would start with 'follow the money'. Given the amount likely involved between multi million dollar yachts, lost treasure and drugs, I needed to better understand what you do with that much cash. I called my old buddy Matt Divine given his work in the investigative world and ran my idea by him.

"Matt, if I had a bunch of cash or gems that I came by let's say under suspicious circumstances, how would I clean that up and make it legit?"

"Finn, what have you gotten yourself into?"

Did I mention that Matt was a smart guy?

To which I replied, "this is purely hypothetical at this point but I may have a little problem down here that involves my ex wife."

He laughed, "Why am I not surprised. What do you

need?"

I laid out my theory to him.

"Finn there are many ways to launder money including everything from smurfing and trade-based invoicing to black salaries or round tripping?

"Jesus Matt, what is smurfing?"

"Actually based on what you suspect I think smurfing is unlikely as it involves breaking large deposits into small amounts and say, buying money orders to then deposit in order to avoid banking regulations. I think round tripping is more likely if you are talking large amounts."

"Ok I'll bite. What is round tripping?"

"That is a bit more complicated but the basics are cash is shipped out of the country and deposited in a offshore foreign corporation that you control through cutouts, preferably in a tax haven where minimal records are kept. That corporation then makes a foreign direct investment exempt from taxation into your corporation in the US."

"Bingo," I replied. So what you are saying is if I control a foreign company offshore, I can make payments to that company for services rendered, such as consulting and in turn they can make an investment in my company or project. I get clean money from them and they get cash without a lot of records."

"Actually that is more of a combination of trade based laundering with inflated invoices combined with round tripping but you get the idea," Matt said.

"Matt you are a life saver, I owe you!" I hung up.

~ ~ ~

I could see light at the end of the tunnel now that I had a working theory. Linebush is collecting sunken treasure from the old family stash whenever he needs cash. He goes to an off shore corporation - read wealthy Nicaraguan farmer - who invests in one of his projects using cash from the drug trade. Linebush pays the wealthy farmer back with the gold. The accountant gets suspicious when these investments are getting deposited into company accounts run by Eddie. He confronts Linebush who points out that the accountant has been an unwitting part of this little scheme so the accountant decides it is a good idea to get out of town with his family.

The wealthy farmer, for some reason, is not getting paid so he kidnaps Linebush to get his money.

I still don't know were Cross fits in this, so maybe it doesn't hang together perfectly but it feels close.

My next step was to have a little chat with my old buddy Eddie Ransom, the money guy.

I called Eddie on his cell and asked if he was doing anything. He seemed distracted but agreed to meet me at Schooner Wharf near his condo in twenty minutes when I asked him for his help with a little financial problem I was having. *Not the whole truth but close.*

I gave Crutch a nudge to wake him up and we headed out of the VFW and off to Schooners on the scooter.

~ ~ ~

I was beginning to feel a time crunch given the deadline set by Ortega and needed to push a few buttons to move things along. I had suggested a public place given what I was about to suggest to him and after my last experience of almost getting run down, I was feeling a bit of a target on my back.

Eddie sauntered in about five minutes after I arrived and came over to my table. We ordered a couple of Stellas and I lit one of Miguel's hand rolled cigars. Eddie made a bit of small talk then asked what was so urgent that it couldn't wait till morning.

"Eddie I have a problem that I am trying to think through and need someone with your background."

Eddie looked a bit puzzled but said anything he could do to help he would do. I decided to stick close to the truth and see where it led. "Eddie first of all this needs to be between us, okay?"

He nodded and said, "Of course."

"Eddie, I am working a case and something has come up that is outside of my expertise. Let's say, and this is just hypothetical, a client is diving out toward Dry Tortuga and finds some gold bullion. He would like to convert it to cash. Do you have any idea how he might do be able to do this?"

He paused then said, "Finn, this is a very tricky area. Technically this is considered treasure and depending on the origin of it, he may owe the state of Florida something, it may belong to the county of origin, if it is say, the Spanish Government and if it is lost bullion."

"Eddie, here is the deal, I heard a rumor that the Linebush family found a treasure many years ago. If it is true, how would they dispose of it?"

Slowly he replied, "Finn, with the new restrictions and tracking on cash, it is almost impossible to easily get rid of gold or jewels like a treasure. Large sums of cash need to be declared and rare coins or old Spanish bullion are easily traced to the ship or the mine they came from."

"Eddie, you have been the Linebush broker for many years and they helped you set up your advisory business. Wade was your partner and you avoided jail in his Ponzi scheme. After Wade went to jail, you were the one in the money business who owed them. You are in a position to know about investments from offshore corporations that might be used for say bonding purposes on different projects they are working on or for partnerships in projects they are developing." I took a breath.

Eddie seemed to visibly shrink with the mention of bonding and tried to recover with bluster.

"Finn you know you are an asshole," he stammered. "If you say any of this in public, I will sue you for slander, and defamation," he spit out. "You have no proof at all and if you think I will just roll over, you are an idiot!" With that, he stormed off leaving me with the bill for the beers.

Well that was interesting. It looked like I was going to have to find myself a new broker. But waste not, want not, so I finished both beers and headed out. What I didn't know was how close I was to the truth about Eddie and also how far off....

~ ~ ~

Sometimes with a case you just have to keep shaking the tree until fruit falls from one branch or another. Often the weakest limb is a good place to start. I thought it might be time to find Squeaky and shake him up. As I left Schooners I noticed a blue pick up in the parking lot down the lane so I decided to wander over. Could I be getting this lucky in my old age?

The windows were cracked open and I couldn't help noticing the smell of stale sweat and cigarettes emanating from the interior. The loud snoring gave me another hint. I peered in and the figure curled around a rum bottle had to be Squeaky. I took a quick look at the rear bumper and saw the bumper sticker I so clearly remembered.

I banged on the side of the truck, opened the pickup door and grabbed him by the arm. The bottle fell empty to the floorboards and he flailed around as I dragged him out of the seat. His eyes began to focus and I could see the recognition begin to show on his face. Even in his current condition he knew he was in trouble.

He tried to run but could barely muster a step or two before falling down. I dragged him around to the back of a shed near the back of Jimmy Buffett's studio building down from Schooners and tapped him gently on the side of his head – well maybe not *so* gently. After all he did try to run me down so one good thump in return for another seemed only fair.

"Squeaky, who put you up to trying to kill me?"

Squeaky lived up to his name and tried to speak but all that came out was a little squeak. I had to laugh. "Don't make me laugh," I said with my imitation of a hard case cop. "Who was it?"

Again a squeak then a slurred, "I don know what you're talkin' bout."

This was the part about interrogation that always stumped me. In movies and television, the hero is always able to beat a confession out of a suspect or shoot them in the knee when they only have twenty-four hours to solve a case. I was down to about thirty-six hours but had a moral compass that was getting in my way.

Squeaky worked for Cross now and Cross knew Squeaky hated Linebush for firing him. It seemed a safe bet that it was Cross who did not want me sniffing around so he probably put Squeaky up to the hit and run.

"OK, Squeaky, I am going to let you go. I'll just let Cross know that you *squeaked* on him ... no sorry, squealed on him," I said muffling a snicker. "I'm sure he will appreciate that little piece of information."

"Wait," he squeaked, "I didn't tell you about him."

"You just did dude, so all I want to know now is why?"

"He didn't tell me why, he just said if I wanted to keep my job I should try to scare you off. I wasn't trying to kill you; just put you in a cast for a while. After all, you cost me two years of my life so I figured if I could fuck you up, it was fair."

I whacked him again and said, "Fuck you. Get out of my sight." He staggered across the street, jumped back in his truck and headed out of the parking lot as I called 911 to report a drunk driver in a dark blue pickup truck with the Florida plate SQUEAKY.

Not really his plate, but they would figure it out. With any luck and his past record it should get him out the picture for at least 30 days. Then again, it *is* Key West where to be safe on the roads you just assume everyone has had one too many. We take defensive driving to a whole new level.

So Cross wants me out of the picture, but why? I had no real evidence that Cross was out to get me, just the forced statement of an impaired low life under threat of injury. That and the rumor that the Linebush and Cross families hate each other. I was back to following the money but at least I had a target if not a map.

CHAPTER NINE

NOW KEY WEST is a small island, only about two by four miles but it offers a lot of options for indulgence. There are almost three hundred restaurants and bars catering to every type of predilection from rum bars to wine bars, historical to dive bars, gay to clothing optional bars and everything in between.

I needed a place to start. Like almost every small town on the gulf coast, drug trafficking is a way of life. The Coast Guard has a large base in Key West and they run daily patrols and work regularly with the DEA trying to slow, if not stop, the flow of cocaine and marijuana into the country. U.S. Customs and Border Protection have flights off the coast looking for smugglers day and night.

Just this past month they seized a hundred plus foot yacht with a Jacuzzi, jet skis, kite boards and six hundred and twenty pounds of cocaine as it docked in Key West. The crew began off loading duffel bags into a pickup truck. CBP grabbed three people in the process including the Captain who had recently been part of a Cuba to Key West swim. The haul was valued at over $5 million.

It seems keeping an over one hundred foot yacht afloat requires more than fuel and a crew.

It was time to pay a visit to my old buddy OJ to see if there were any rumors about Cross and the drug trade, if for no other reason than to eliminate that as a motive.

When I called him, he growled, "Fuck off Finns, I'm busy," and hung up. As you have probably gathered we have a deep and abiding respect for each other.

I called him back. "Fuck you OJ" and I hung up.

Square Grouper

OK, so I needed to look elsewhere. I had at this point a mild buzz on so I needed to slow down on the booze. I decided a virgin Bloody Mary and a visit to Cindy at Southernmost Café was in order. Crutch and I hopped on my scooter, hustled down Truman, and parked by Southernmost House. Crutch was off the scooter in a flash and racing to the bar for his feed of treats from the bar staff.

He performed his usual bag of tricks including a high five, low five, roll over and finally his showstopper - balancing a cookie on his nose until I tell him he can have it. Then he shakes his head and catches the treat before it hits the ground. After getting treats from almost every member of the bar staff for each performance, I tell him he is a shameless hustler, at which point he buries his snout in his paws and looks to all the world like he is ashamed. It always gets a laugh and a final round of treats.

After the show, I took Cindy aside and asked her if she knows anyone in town who is tapped into the drug trade. To a Key West bartender that is like asking, "Do you know how to make a Bloody Mary?" Cindy was a bit taken aback until I explained that I needed to talk to someone about a case I was working on.

Now Cindy is an old friend but she also knows that talking to a cop even a retired one can be a potential problem. After a discreet shrug she said, "Finn I like you," which was news to me, "but I don't know anyone who might know anything about the local drug trade. I suggest you head back toward Lower Duval where the action is and talk to some of the *ladies* along the way.

Now Key West at one time was truly a *Fish, Fuck and Fight* town. Even in the seventies, rumor has it if you didn't bring a gun into a bar they gave you one when you entered. The shrimpers and the swabbies would bang heads most nights and sensible folk would lay low. Over time, the shrimp boat harbor was moved from Garrison Bight out to Stock Island, the Navy began to reduce its presence and the town fathers, looking for another source of income began cleaning things up for tourists.

Lower Duval became a tourist mecca: t-shirt shops selling threadbare cotton shirts featuring tasteless sayings, cigar shops where you could sample the wares, and bars with vague associations to Hemingway and Tennessee Williams. A lot of the seedier elements became more low key but you could still find a down-on-her-luck *lady* offering a *bit on the side* for the right price.

I decided a bit of exercise walking up Duval would be good for Crutch, so favoring my ankle, I limped up the street stopping at the first house to offer *female companionship*. On a side note, in Key West, a word of caution, you need to be careful that your *female* companion is indeed female. I needed to spend a few minutes meeting with the girls and observing them dance to be sure I was talking to the right gender. It was all in the name of investigative research of course.

After selecting a very thin, somewhat jittery blond named Trixie, no really that's her name at least that's what she claimed. From her accent she sounded eastern European so maybe it was Trixanna originally. I asked her for a private dance and once ensconced in a small room with a single bed she invited me to sit on the bed and began to slowly remove my shirt... . well you get the idea. It became clear that if I didn't get to the questions soon I might become distracted so I asked her about getting drugs. At first she was a bit reticent but after a hundred dollar tip, she offered that for the kind of information I was looking for I should talk to Billy at the Green Parrot.

The Green Parrot is basically a tourist bar made famous as the Southernmost bar on the A1A. My new friend Trixie explained that Billy was a regular at the bar who could hook me up with whatever I needed. I thanked Trixie for the show, and somewhat reluctantly skipping the follow-on services the place is famous for. I buttoned my shirt and got out for only $300 bucks. Not bad given the establishment's reputation for shall we say *screwing the clientele.*

The Green Parrot is a favorite place for tourists and locals looking for great music and popcorn. It is one of the last real bars in Key West, famous for great blues bands who come to town from all over the country. *Sound Check* at six o'clock on Friday and Sunday afternoons are the best times to find locals who are avoiding the tourists. It was just about time for the 6 o'clock show so it would be a good time to find Billy. A crowd favorite band, Jimbo Mathus with their gutbucket North Mississippi Juke Joint Blues, was pounding on stage. One patron described it as "like a Cadillac driving off a cliff".

It turned out Billy was not hard to find. With Trixie's description in mind, he was the one with the long blonde ponytail and the tattoo of a multi-colored hookah on his right arm. I eased onto the seat next to him at the bar and shouted over the band's version of Who Do You Love.

"Trixie, said you were a guy I needed to meet."

To which he replied continuing to stare at the band, "Trixie who?"

"Trixie with her lips on your Hookah." I smiled.

He was smiling when he turned to face me, then he started to bolt. He must have been carrying and thought I was still a cop. I guess you never really lose the look.

With my ankle still wrapped and sore, I was not going to chase him down but Crutch's leash tangled between my stool and his, hampering his quick getaway. Crutch growled as Billy hit the floor and I bent down to help him up. A little pressure point under his armpit kept him under control and I told him I was not interested in his stash but was just looking for some information.

I put fifty bucks down on the bar in front of him and ordered two Stellas while he sat back down on the stool eying the bearded face of Ulysses S. Grant.

"Billy, I am looking for information regarding a private matter. If you can help me, there is another fifty in it for you. What do you say?"

He paused and said, "What kind of information?"

I now had him at least nibbling the bait. Now I needed to set the hook and reel him in. "I have a client who is looking to move significant weight and I need a contact for him. He is willing to give five percent to the guy who can hook him up and if I can do it, I will give twenty-five percent of my share to the guy who helps me and facilitates an introduction. That could be you if you are willing to play."

He stared at me and the wheels were turning, more like grinding but at least moving. *Too many big words, I thought*?

"How do I know you are not a cop, setting me up?"

I thought for a moment and realized that saying, "Do I look like a cop?" was probably not going to work.

"Billy, you are obviously a smart guy, and I like that." Okay, so a bit of flattery never hurts.

"As a matter of fact you are right, I use to be a cop until I got fired three years ago. I have been living on a small pension and watching as everybody else seems to be making a buck and I am living on shit. I just want a piece of the action."

"Fifty/fifty," he said. This guy was tough.

I set the hook. "Forty/sixty after the first payment."

He paused and said, "How much weight are we talking about?"

"My client wants to move a hundred kilos a month and does not want to make waves."

The wheels were turning again as he was trying to figure out his share. Math was clearly not his strong suit.

"Your share would be forty percent of twelve thousand, five hundred dollars or five thousand a month."

Now he paused and was picturing a fully rigged forty-foot Sportfisher in his mind.

"Ok," he said. "But not here. Meet me at Pussy Galore on Caroline at one o'clock. And come alone." At which point he held out his hand and said, "Give me my other fifty."

I smiled. "You'll get it when we meet later." I then turned and left him to pay the bar tab from the first fifty on the bar.

~ ~ ~

I now had a few hours to kill but at least I had a lead. Pussy Galore, like the name implies, is another of the local places where lonely gentleman can find company for a fee. Ostensibly a dance parlor, rumor has it that *happy endings* can be had for an additional stipend. Not so nominal if you make the mistake of giving them a credit card. It is located in a slightly run down Victorian Gingerbread house near Grinnell and Caroline and at one in the morning it is not the best place to be if you are alone.

If I was connecting with a real player, it could get hairy. This could be seen by them as an opportunity or it could be seen as a threat. Who was this mysterious client who was bringing in this much weight? I needed a story.

If Cross was the distributor, Billy was going to lead me to, then I needed a plausible reason for my transition from cop and ex-husband/son-in-law of Linebush to newly minted drug middle man. Also, I needed back up and they would know all the local folks.

I called Matt Divine and found him stuck in traffic on Hwy 1 out of Miami heading to Islamadora for a long weekend of R and R.

After a few pleasantries and a bad joke about two hookers and a Rabbi I got to the point. "Matt, I'm looking for a little back up on a case I am working and wondered if you could spare a few hours tonight in Key West."

He paused and asked, "What do you need?"

I briefly explained my plan and after a few questions he said, "Ok it sounds like fun. I can be there in two hours if the traffic lightens up."

I thanked him and said, "Meet me at Café Marquesa on Simonton and I'll buy you a late dinner. We can go over the logistics then. I'll be at the bar at 10:30." He agreed and hung up.

~ ~ ~

Now more about my friend Matt is in order. Matt is one of those rare human beings who not only will have your back but if necessary will take a bullet for you. A Navy SEAL instructor and Honor Man of his BUD/S Class, he served in places that would scare the crap out of even most SEALs. When he jokes, "If I told you I would have to kill you," you actually believe him.

At five-foot-ten and in his mid-fifties, he has the body of a twenty-five-year-old and can still do twenty dead hang pullups without even breaking a sweat. He is a true warrior, yet is quiet and reserved when you meet him. I have only seen him under threat once in a potential street fight one evening coming out of a bar in San Diego. It was like someone threw a switch and he became the scariest dude I have ever seen.

As if by magic, Matt was suddenly in the asshole's face, literally nose to nose. The loudmouthed drunk looked into Matt's eyes, paused, seemed to sober up, and slowly backed away. Matt quietly waited until the guy moved off and then turned to me. For a split second I saw what this guy must have seen.

The emptiness in his eyes was a black hole and revealed a bottomless pit of pain and the potential for extreme violence. Then he smiled and was back to just my friend. Whatever far away place he went to must have been truly dark for it was as if he was Jekyll and Hyde.

~ ~ ~

With Matt on his way, and a plan in place, I decided to get Crutch home, fed and watered then catch a couple of hours sleep before the evening's festivities got started.

The alarm clock in my head woke me at 10:00 and after a quick shower, I took the scooter and was at the Marquesa right at 10:30. It's a small island.

Given that tonight could get a little hairy, I ordered a glass of Zin and waited for Matt. About ten forty five, he came in cursing under his breath about the fucking traffic and ordered a martini ice cold no vermouth with a twist. I have seen him drink five of these and never even slur a word.

We took a table away from the windows and after slipping the waiter fifty bucks to convince the chef to feed us. We ordered dinner and I walked through the plan, knowing that no plan survives first contact with the enemy.

"Matt, for this meeting, you are working for an Afghani drug exporter as his local muscle. Here is your muscle shirt."

He had to laugh as I handed him a wife beater in a small bag. The smile faded as he felt the weight of the bag and at a glance spotted my H&K USP40 under the shirt. Rather than comment, he listened intently as I described the plan.

"The story is your contact is looking to expand and move major weight into the U.S. He is giving you the chance to be the primary U.S. contact. You are a

66

dishonorably discharged Green Beret who was moving drugs during two tours of duty in *The Suck* as we called Iraq. You met the seller then and he reestablished contact with you once you returned to the U.S."

It is a hard story to check given the long distance and difficulty of getting info out of the military.

"You contacted me as a guy you knew in the *Sand Box* and who had been fired as a cop in Key West. You thought I might know a distributor on the east coast to add to your network."

He had only four questions: "What is the objective; what are my actions; what are the ROE's (Rules of engagements) and what are my orders?"

I love working with professionals and I outlined the plan. "My client, if you want to call him that, is a suspected Nicaraguan drug dealer named Ortega who has kidnapped my ex-wife Courtney and her father. He has given me seventy-two hours to recover money he says he gave to the father to invest or he will put serious hurt on my ex and he has already shot her father in the leg."

After a breath, I continued, "A local low life tried to run me down yesterday as I was shaking the bushes, pun intended. It turns out he is working for the Cross family. They are another local family who I understand are in the *pharmaceutical business*. You know there are three basic problems in the drug business: getting the drugs into the country; distributing them in the country; and getting the cash out of the country."

Matt continued to listen intently while I told him what I know. "Ortega has a source of drug supply and he has kidnapped Linebush. Eddie Ransom, a financial advisor to Linebush met recently with Peter Cross, the son of Nikos Cross. Wade Linebush was Eddie's business partner and I busted Wade for running a Ponzi scheme.

Then I moved on to tell Matt what I suspected. "Cross

using this lowlife Squeaky appears to have tried to run me down as a way to get me out of the picture or at least to get me to back away. Linebush may have a way to get Spanish treasure his family found many years ago from a sunken ship turning it into cash."

I went on to outline my laundry list of questions. "Why did Ortega kidnap Linebush? Who is distributing drugs and how does Ortega get his money out? Where does Cross fit in this puzzle? And what do I know that would cause him to try and slow down the investigation?"

Matt knew right away that all I was trying to do was stir the pot and see what bubbled to the surface. He paused for a minute then simply said, "Actions and orders?"

Don't you love a pro?

"You are my back up and muscle for now. If things get hairy, non-lethal force is okay. If the opportunity arises a broken wrist or blown knee is okay to make a point that we are serious. Time is important so we need to move things along as I am down to less than 36 hours."

"Got it."

As we left the restaurant he went to the men's room and slipped on the wife beater, tucked the USP 40 into his waistband and we took his car and headed for the rendezvous. It is hard to look like a tough pair of drug dealers riding on my scooter.

We parked a block from Caroline about midnight and walked up the street looking over the lay of the land. It was quiet and I had to wonder how the girls at Pussy Galore would make a buck with this lack of foot traffic.

Matt did his best impression of a future patron as we strolled along and we both noted the two guys sitting in a parked car in the lot next to the plumbing store on Grinnell. In Key West that could mean a lot of different things, from a couple of college kids getting up the courage to visit the ladies to a gay couple getting to know each other. We needed to keep them in mind in the event that they were there as back up for our contact this evening.

With about forty minutes to kill we walked over to Half Shell Raw Bar for a beer and a half dozen oysters, we finalized details about our characters, reviewed the plan. About five to one we left the bar.

As we walked past Harpoon Harry's, a great breakfast place on the corner, I spotted Billy walking slowly along Caroline accompanied by a face and bandaged wrist I recognized. Now this was going to be interesting. Kids today I thought.

"Well, hello Gorilla boy!" I smiled.

CHAPTER TEN

LESLIE, THE STEROID PUMPED body man for Peter Cross, walked up to me but was looking at Matt.

"Billy said come alone," he grunted.

"What? No good to see you, Finn. Long time no see?"

"Don't push your luck asshole, you got lucky last time."

I turned to Billy, "So this guy is the muscle Billy?, where's Peter?"

"First we need to frisk you Finn and your friend too."

I nodded and Leslie stepped in and was a little rough with the search but I took it. When he tried to search Matt, he winced and pretended it hurt.

Leslie laughed. "Some back up Finn. You brought your sister?"

Then he found the gun and stopped laughing.

Leslie pocketed it and Matt said quietly, "I'm gonna want that back."

Now anyone with half a brain would have heard the menace in his voice but Leslie just sneered, "You can try to take it back when we're all done, Nancy."

At this point, the doors of the car in the parking lot opened up and the two men got out. Peter was no surprise but the other one was an unknown. They came over and Matt coughed.

I turned to him and it was clear he recognized the second man if not by name, then by type. It looked like Peter had upgraded his protection since our encounter the day before.

"Hello, Finn," said Peter slowly.

"Hello Peter," I mimicked.

"So Finn, Billy tells me you have some new friends and you are looking to get into the import business."

I looked at Peter and asked, "Before we start, who is you new muscle?"

"I'll show you mine, if you show me yours," he snickered.

"Peter, Peter, Peter," I said slowly. "If you keep trying to prove you have a bigger dick than I do, then this is going to be a very disappointing meeting for you."

"Fuck you Finn."

His muscle head touched his arm and said, "My friends call me Georgi. My enemies," he paused for emphasis, "avoid me." He smiled to reveal a big gold tooth in front.

Really?

A bit melodramatic I thought but he looked built to deliver. His eastern European accent caused him to sound like a James Bond bad guy.

"Well, Georgi, I hope we can be friends." I smiled and offered my hand which he ignored.

"Enough Finn," said Peter. "Who's your girlfriend?"

Matt said in a timid, academic voice, "My name is Johnson. I represent interests in Afghanistan who were looking to export products to the U.S. and need a capable partner. Mr. Pilar is an old acquaintance who offered to make an introduction. If he is mistaken that you are such potential partners, then we can part friends and move on."

He sounded like an accountant being challenged by an IRS agent and had a bit of a quiver in his voice.

Peter seemed to be thinking and finally said, "Mr. Johnson, while your choice of friends is questionable, I may be able to help you."

To which Matt replied, "Excellent, perhaps we can discuss your business terms over lunch tomorrow?"

Peter decided to push things a little and said, "Before

we get started Mr. Johnson, you need to understand that we have no interest in dealing with Finn. We will not do any business as long as he is involved."

Peter looked at me and smiled. I smiled back.

At this point, Leslie decided it was time for a little payback and added emphasis to Peter's comments. He pushed me from the side telling me to piss off.

I turned to face him, "You know, Gorilla boy, the cafe was obviously not enough of a lesson for you."

Georgi seemed to decide to let this play out and stepped back.

Leslie stood to his full height of about six four, cracked his neck, raised his fists into a fighter's stance and tried to surprise me with a kick.

Now the thing you need to understand about muscle heads is they often have a lot of bulk that can be intimidating but it also makes them slow. The easiest thing to do is simply step back from the kick, let it pop in front of you, then help it along by lifting the foot up using his momentum until the rest of him goes down on his back.

Leslie went down hard but seemed to take it well and was back on his feet quickly.

I smiled at Leslie and said, "Come on asshole, let's finish this now so I can get to my Pilates class."

With that, he tried a roundhouse swing with his good hand. This time I stepped into it, lowered my head and caught it just above my forehead. This is probably the hardest bone in your body and while a tough fighter can ring your bell, they usually shatter their hand. I am sure they heard Leslie squeal to Mallory Square as the bones in his hand became fragments.

I stepped back, shook my head to clear the fog and caught a flash out of the corner of my eye as Georgi was stepping in to take Leslie's spot.

Suddenly Matt caught hold of Peter and said, "Georgi,

before you decide to commit to this little fracas, you may want to make sure your boss is in one piece," his voice quiet and calm. Georgi turned and saw Matt holding the tip of a pen to Peter's carotid artery in his neck, squirming on his tiptoes with Matt's arm around his neck.

I hooked one foot behind Leslie's ankle and drove my other foot sideways against the knee hearing a nasty pop as it snapped. Leslie screamed and collapsed with a shattered knee and hand in addition to the wrist I broke the other day.

Georgi realized that with Peter at risk, he needed to fix that first before getting to me but it became apparent that Matt was more than a simple accountant. Georgi put up his hands and backed up to show he was not a threat and waited.

I turned to Matt and said, "Mr. Johnson I think you need to let Peter breathe or we will have to go looking for a new partner."

Matt, slowly released the pressure on Peter and his color improved.

I decided it was time to establish the operating agreements of our relationship. "Peter, I think you need to understand that you are not in charge of this deal. Mr. Johnson has associates who make your boy Georgi seem like a choir boy and they have been in the *export* business since before Columbus discovered America."

I just kept making my point. "Also, he is a product of the finest military training in the world. I suggest you proceed with him to make a deal over lunch and enjoy the profits that can be derived from this arrangement."

At this point Matt aka Mr. Johnson, released Peter.

Then 'Mr. Johnson' began, "We need to know a couple of things. We will take care of the import function but we would like to know more about your export of the cash."

Peter was still trying to catch his breath and Georgi

was very still, trying to assess Matt.

Finally Georgi said, "That is my department."

"I'm sorry, but who are you, and how do you do that?" I asked.

At this point information began to flow.

"For a fee, Mr. Cross uses us to handle any cash investments he is looking to place overseas in safe locations."

That's a different way to describe money laundering but when in Rome ... .

"Who is us?" I inquired and Georgi simply said, "My colleagues."

This was going nowhere but I figured it was enough to start and decided to move to the next level.

"How does this work?" I asked.

He simply said, "You bring us the cash and while you wait, we make a deposit in a numbered account of your choice for eighty percent of the total. Nice and simple. We take care of getting the cash out of the country and there is no trace of you in the transaction."

I looked at Matt and decided it was time to cut this short.

"Peter," I said, "You and Mr. Johnson make your deal at lunch. I will not be involved from here on in."

With that Matt reached down to Leslie who was on the ground moaning and took the H&K back. "Thank you," he said in a kind gentlemanly voice.

Leslie grunted, "Fuck you."

Matt kicked his knee to make a point and we walked away to the sound of Leslie screaming in the background. I suspect the neighborhood was used to screams of one kind or another.

Matt's first comment as we approached the car was, "I see you still know how to make friends, Finn. What are you doing messing with the Russian Mafia?"

That caught me off guard so I said, "Say what?"

"Geogri is a member of the Russian Mafia and I suspect ex-Spetsnaz by the way he moved. You know how to stir up a hornets nest, dude."

As we got in the car, a couple of pieces fell into place. One of the bodies found recently was tattooed like an eastern European gang member. Is there a connection? The first body was a member of a Salvadorian drug gang. It was beginning to look like I was in the middle of a war between Cross and the Russians versus Linebush and Ortega?

CHAPTER ELEVEN

WE DECIDED TO SWING OVER to Sloppy Joe's for a final late night pop and debrief. We each ordered a Dark and Stormy and I asked Matt if he was open to an R and R weekend in Key West. He glanced at me and said, "Only if you promise me breakfast Bloody Mary's from Cindy and Paella for lunch at El Siboney."

It seemed pretty cheap to me so I agreed.

At this point, I was beginning to think I had a couple of threads but I was running out of time. And besides, why should I care? Having two old bubba families fighting over drugs and money was not really my concern. Courtney and her father, *my clients* hated my guts and I had never really heard of Cross before yesterday. Finally it was beginning to look like the bodies found so far where just part of a turf war.

Where was my dog in this hunt? Speaking of dogs, I should probably get back and take Crutch for his late night fluid adjustment walk.

We polished off our drinks and as we drove to pick up my scooter, I shared my reservations with Matt. As I talked through the situation, it came to me that I was being a bit shallow. Courtney was still my ex-wife and I admit I carry a bit of a torch for her. Squeaky would have run me down but for Crutch barking, Leslie had tried to cripple me twice now and my old friend Eddie turned out to be a crook. Finally, what if Wade was innocent? I had been largely responsible for convicting Wade when it may have been Eddie who had cost me my wife and my job.

I said to Matt, "You know I think I may have an idea. Take the next left onto Truman and lets go pay someone a visit". I explained my plan to Matt as we drove up Truman toward White Street. He was not excited about it but was willing to go along within reason.

We turned onto White and drove past Flagler toward the White Street Pier. At Washington we slowed and turned north onto Von Phister. I had been here several times for parties and knew the layout well. It was one of the newer houses in the area and was set back from the street behind a wall with a beautiful landscape of palms and a large Poinciana tree with bright orange blooms. Most of the lights in the house were out but a second floor light was still on.

We parked about a block down the street and walked back and down through some mango trees by a neighbor's house. We made quick work of the wall and settled onto the back patio by the pool to look for any alarms. After a careful inspection of the windows we could find no sign of any security so I simply lifted the back patio door up and off the track and we stepped into the house.

"The sounds from the second floor left little doubt that *our host* was engaged in something other than watching Conan on TV.

"Ohh fuck me hard ... Yes, yesss, oh fuck yesssss!"

I turned to Matt and whispered, "Sounds like we are going to interrupt someone's happy ending." But there really was no reason to whisper. We could have been a marching band entering the house and we would not have been heard above the noise from the bedroom.

Given our host, I thought it might be interesting to have some evidence of this little tryst so as we crept up the stairs, I pulled out my cell phone and put it on video then quietly opened the door.

I am not sure what I expected but I was truly shocked by the sight of Eddie dressed in a frilly green tutu on his hands and knees on the queen size bed. Peter was kneeling behind him banging away with an erection the size of a ... well, you get the idea. Peter hadn't wasted any time getting over to his lover's place after out meeting.

I almost forgot the video trying not to laugh before they figured out they had company. They immediately scrambled to cover up but got caught up in the sheets and fell off the bed as I continued to video.

"Well, this is awkward guys," I began.

Eddie, trying to regain some dignity sputtered, "What the fuck are you doing in my house?"

To which I replied, "Well we heard what you were up to, so to speak," and smiled.

"Finn, you asshole, I am going to sue for everything you're worth."

"Please do Eddie. I can see the headlines in the Key West Citizen, *Private Dick Charged for Breaking in on a Private Peter Party*. The twitter sphere will go wild."

Even Matt laughed at that one.

My original plan was to break in on Eddie and waterboard him to tell us what was going on, but this latest development gave us plenty of leverage.

I decided to separate the two of them before they could make up a story but keep them naked. People always feel a lot more vulnerable when they are naked. Given the tutu I figured there had to be rope somewhere in the room and after a few seconds, I found some silk ties in the bedside table. I tied up Eddie's hands behind his back, then Peter's.

"Matt, you take Peter and use this room, I will take Eddie down to the main floor. I expect the neighbors are used to screams coming from here so noise should not be a problem. You can kill him if you need to and we can take care of the bodies later."

Matt looked at me a little askance but kept it to himself as he knew I was only bluffing.

I dragged Eddie to his feet and we walked down the stairs to the living room. I drew the blinds and dropped him down on the sofa.

"Eddie, Eddie, Eddie," I slowly began.

"Look, Finn, I don't have to mention your breaking and entering to anyone. You can just walk away and I won't say a word."

"Eddie, I don't think you get it," I replied with a grin. "You have a serious problem and the only way to fix it is to talk to me."

"No Finn, *you* don't get it. This is Key West. Being gay is not a big deal. It's almost a benefit."

"Eddie, I don't give a shit about your sexual orientation or your preference for tutus. Your choice of partner is another thing."

"I expect that your financial planning business might suffer if this video shows up on You Tube. My phone was set to video so I have you live and in color."

Now it was time to get down to business. "Here is what I know: one, you or Cross sent Squeaky to run me down; two, you are having sex with the Peter Cross who is married to my ex-wife; three, you manage money for Roger Linebush; four, your ex-partner was Wade Linebush who went to jail for his part in a Ponzi scheme; five, Peter's new bodyguard is an ex-Russian Spetznaz commando and one of the bodies that showed up recently was also Russian Special Forces; *I think anyway*. And finally, the best one is that you like to have gay sex wearing a Tutu."

I could tell he was really taking all this information in and doing a fast compute of what I was saying. "Eddie, What I think is you have been telling tales out of school on Linebush to your lover Peter. I think my friend who is a very dangerous guy, will learn more about what those are and you will be screwed, and not in the way you seem to enjoy."

Now I could see a hint of a squirm. "I think you got

caught short of cash after Wade went to jail because you have been living beyond your means. You went to Cross who is a mortal enemy of Linebush and asked for help. Cross offered to help you by funneling money through you that he needed laundered from his drug business if you would get Courtney to marry his *rainbow loving son.*"

I was just making this stuff up on the fly but the pieces sort of fit. Eddie immediately denied everything, which was not unexpected, but I pushed him.

"Look Eddie, with these pictures and what I have on Squeaky and what he told me, I can at least get the police to look into it. I expect a financial analysis or an SEC audit of your advisory service would be interesting and make a lot of local dignitaries upset. Tell me where I am wrong."

"Fuck you Finn, you don't know shit." So much for Mr. Nice Guy.

"Ok Eddie, time for Plan B."

I asked him to stand up from the sofa and given that his hands were tied behind his back, he had to lean over and as he did I caught him with a solid knee to the face that broke his nose and caused him to pass out.

"Boy Eddie, your buddy Peter is really into the rough stuff," I said to myself as I lifted him off the floor, onto my shoulder and walked into the kitchen.

I remembered that Eddie had a really nice kitchen, all stainless steel and glass with a beautiful Wolf gas range with instant-on burners and a nice grill on one side to cook steaks and chicken. Did I mention that I like to cook? I really love this range. Range envy you might call it.

I hefted Eddie up on the range and sat him up on grill. He was still pretty groggy so I rooted around in the kitchen drawers until I found some duck tape. *Every kitchen has duct tape and if it doesn't, it should.* I taped his legs to the handle of the oven and taped the oven closed so he could not run but could only sit or stand. I threw some water into his face and as he came around he looked very confused.

"Eddie, I think it is important for you to understand that I don't have a lot of time."

"Wha ... th ... fuc ..." he muttered looking down as he realized he was sitting on the stove.

I turned on one of the burners and it flared beside him.

"Nooooooo!" he cried.

"Eddie, it is time to talk or your ass is going to have grill marks on it like a rare steak. Not to mention your balls."

"You wouldn't dare," he cried so I fired up the grill on low and he screamed.

I turned it off and he kept screaming as it cooled down.

"Finn, I don't know what you want," he sobbed so I fired up the grill again and this time on medium. These gas ranges are great for producing instant heat.

He stood up on his toes with his knees taped to the oven handle. I pushed him back and he screamed. This time you could smell his butt. Well at least burning flesh. He stood up again.

"Eddie, your future partners are really going to love those little grill marks."

"Alright, alright. Look Finn this is not about you, it's about Linebush."

Now that was an interesting comment. "Why would I think it was about me?"

"Squeaky tried to run you down, that's why."

"Oh, right," and I pushed him back onto the grill again and he screamed. "Enough, I'll tell you what you want to know."

"So start talking."

"Listen Finn, this is about Linebush cutting into

Cross's business. Cross has had a sweet deal for a long time, bringing in drugs through Key West and the Russians laundering the money. I handle the investments and everybody wins. When you busted Wade for his Ponzi deal, old man Linebush had to find another source of cash to handle his losses and finish the construction projects or he would have gone broke."

"And Ortega?" I queried.

"Linebush approached Ortega for cash and Ortega was bringing in drugs and it cut into Cross's and the Russians' deals. The Russians lost it and sent Ortega a message. Ortega then hit one of the Russian guys and now we have war."

I thought about this for a minute and then asked, "So why would Ortega kidnap Linebush and Courtney?"

"I don't know, it makes no sense to me."

I didn't buy it so I gave him a little push and he screamed even before he hit the grill. "I don't believe you, so talk or your ass is going to be well done, and not in a good way."

"Finn, I don't know for sure," he sniffed. "I think Linebush is in over his head and owes Ortega money so he is trying to collect it using you."

"So why try to run me down?" It seemed a logical question.

"Cross figured if you were out of the picture, you couldn't help Linebush find Daniels and pay back Ortega so he would finish Linebush off for us. Problem solved."

This story was hanging together and at this point Matt walked in and started laughing. Eddie looked pitiful standing on his toes taped to the stove. It would make quite a quirky Facebook photo.

"One last question Eddie, where does Daniels the CFO fit in this and where is he?"

"Daniels discovered that we were skimming funds

from Linebush's account to pay back Cross for the money Wade stole so he went to Linebush. When Cross killed Ortega's man, I think Daniels took off thinking he might be next. I don't know were he is."

I turned off the stove and told Eddie once it cooled down he could sit down. I suggested Neosporin for his butt and asked Matt to grab Peter and we would take him with us. "We can let him go on Duval and he can walk back to free Eddie."

"Eddie, I am keeping the video as a souvenir in the event that you chose to discuss this evening with anyone."

The three of us left him standing taped to the stove and drove to Duval and Greene downtown to let Peter off. It would take him about half hour to get back to free Eddie as long as he wasn't arrested first.

Unfortunately, we were no closer to tracking down the money and getting Linebush and Courtney released. Time was running out.

We drove back to my place and by the time we got back two of Crutches three legs were crossed so I took him for a short walk. Matt cracked a bottle of Pilar Rum and poured two snifters to lubricate our debrief of Matt's *conversation* with Peter.

It turned out Peter pretty much confirmed Eddie's story.

Old Man Cross was pissed with Linebush for horning in on his drug trade. They went after one of his enforcers to send a message and Linebush responded with going after one of the Russians. But he didn't know why Ortega kidnapped Linebush.

The only added piece that Peter knew was his father was making a run out to the Dry Tortugas tomorrow to pick up a shipment of cocaine to bring back to the island for distribution tomorrow night. After our late night run in with Peter, I didn't expect our imaginary drug deal with

Peter would happen and Cross was going to be looking to shut us down. Things were getting more complicated by the minute.

It was time to pay old man Cross a late night visit before Peter talked to him. It was time to take the fight to him.

CHAPTER TWELVE

I GRABBED MY DIVE GEAR from the shed, checked the tanks and we hopped back in Matt's car, our drinks untouched. We headed for the Navy pier and with Matt as a lookout, I slipped over the side of the Outer Mole into the dark waters and began to swim out toward Sunset Key. This is a very treacherous channel when the tides are running and several people get washed out to sea each year. The tide was slack and the moon was a sliver in the western sky, the tropical waters were warm and the stars blinked on and off as clouds drifted by.

As I submerged, I was reminded of the many nights in training for Explosive Ordinance Disposal (EOD) off Coronado with the difference being the Draegar Rigs and fifty-eight degree waters. Actually fifty-eight degrees is a really big difference from the Key's eighty degrees when you think about it. *I know which one I prefer.*

At four thirty in the morning there was not much traffic in the channel. During the day it was like the 405 freeway in LA with Fury boats headed out parasailing, sun burned tourists on jet skis forming a staggered line out into the ocean, catamarans full of rum punch drunk land lubbers on lunch time booze cruises and the occasional Coast Guard or Navy patrol boat cruising by.

Cross's home was a big yellow Victorian knockoff on the eastern edge of Sunset Key, right on the channel. It did not have great views as the cheap bastard didn't want to pay for the full sunset. He would be heading out tomorrow evening making a run toward Dry Tortuga and I wanted to leave him a small gift. One of the benefits of being in Special Ops is you get really comfortable diving at night. If

I could get close to his boat I might be able to figure out how he moved the drugs. Simply loading them on a fast boat was an invitation to get caught by the Coast Guard.

I approached his dock from the blind side at the stern as it floated gently in the calm channel waters. As I swam around the hull under the boat I noticed a section of the hull was molded in an odd shape. At first I thought it might be a go-fast hull design that many boats have today but as I got closer it looked like it could hold a .... *Oh Shit*.

Suddenly the waters surrounding the thirty-foot cigarette boat lit up and I realized I had missed a trip wire set under water behind the boat. I was rusty and would never have missed it had I been ten years younger and had taken time for recon and mission planning.

I slipped deeper under the boat and quickly headed toward a channel marker about two hundred yards off the dock. I resisted the urge to take a quick look back hoping that the system was triggered often enough with false alarms from the occasional tarpon grazing by for cast-off chum. The channel marker would give me a chance to look back to see if a proper search was being made of the boat.

As I feared, Cross's ex-Ranger gorilla Leslie came slowly down from the house and was doing a hobble around the dock. The good news was like most Rangers, he was not a big *get-in-the-water-at-4-a.m.* kind of guy. Also given his broken wrist, nose, hand and a cast on his knee he was not going to hop in the water on spec. Seeing nothing unusual he did a scan of the area including a night vision look out toward the channel marker and decided all was well. *Rangers!*

That was when I spotted Georgi the Russian Spetsnaz guard on the beach with a silenced Draganov SVD. The Draganov is a high-powered semi-automatic gas-operated sniper rifle of Soviet design that in the right hands, is deadly at up to almost fifteen hundred yards. If he spotted

Matt on the mole, Matt was toast.

I pulled a flare from my belt and from behind the marker I fired it toward the beach to light up the shooter. The flare should signal Matt to take cover and blind at least Leslie with his night vision goggles.

A round from the Draganov hit the channel marker where my head had been a split second before I dove back under the warm waters. *Too close for comfort.*

I figured Matt would have seen the flare and stayed low behind the power boxes on the pier. I headed for the harbor entrance by the Westin Pier. It was empty except for the parked jet skis, parasailing boats plus a couple of fifty-foot Sport Fishing boats and the booze cruise catamarans all moored for the night.

I stripped off my dive gear and stashed it in the bushes by the Westin to get later in the morning and looked over to the Outer Mole pier for any sign of Matt. He scared me half to death when he whispered in my ear. "You're getting careless Finn. If I had been the Russian, you would have been fish food by now."

How he had gotten from the mole to the Westin so quick was a mystery. He had snuck up on me to make the point and I agreed it was careless. I really was slipping. We had less than 24 hours left to get Courtney and her father back and I didn't need Cross complicating things.

~ ~ ~

The sun was just breaking over the horizon off South Beach as Matt and I got back to Catherine Street. We needed sleep and some time to think. Crutch barely registered my arrival, opened one eye and immediately went back to sleep. Matt made some calls while I crashed for three hours. I woke starving and found Matt in the kitchen cooking eggs and bacon. After food and three cups of coffee, I took Crutch for his morning pee.

We then hopped into Matt's car and went to retrieve

my dive gear and scooter. Using my binoculars, I looked over to Sunset Key and it was clear that Cross's go-fast boat was gone. I had missed out on giving him a nasty surprise last night thanks to his security system. And what the hell was that weird shaped hull designed to do on that boat anyway?

With eight hours to go to meet the deadline Ortega gave me to find Daniels, I was pretty much screwed. I was no closer to finding him and unlike the hero in dime novels that now sell for about ten bucks, I had no clue.

Then it hit me, I am looking at the wrong end of this puzzle.

~ ~ ~

It was a bit late but I thought with luck I might catch my friend Lee over at the White Tarpon. Lee owned a boat that he moored in a slip off A & B Lobster House and had coffee most mornings with an eclectic group of Key West locals. I found him chatting with a couple of other regulars and asked if he had a second to help with a little problem.

Lee is a retired owner of a lighting company who loves to hang out in Key West. It has been said that if you had to put together a team to get anything done from launching a rocket from Antarctica to building a bridge in Zimbabwe, you could find all the talent you needed among retirees in Key West. Lee had been kicking around in the waters off Key West for thirty years and there was nothing he didn't know about them.

"Lee, I am trying to find a big yacht, blue hull, chopper on the back that was here a few days ago and left last Tuesday. It is a Feadship going by the name of ..."

"*Ciao Bella*?" he replied. "Yea, I saw the boat."

"Is there any way to track it down, on the QT?"

"I thought you would have a hard question for me," said Lee. "That question is one *Dijon* could answer." *Dijon* is his Yellow Labradoodle. Lee is witty like that.

I just stared at him with a blank puppy face in hopes that he would get *Dijon* over to answer.

He sighed and said, "Come over to the boat and I will educate you." And with that, we walked over to his Broward 65' and went into the salon. He pulled up his computer and I was expecting *Dijon* to work the keys but alas...

"If you want to find most private yachts in the world you can. Just Google *Marinetraffic.com* and enter the name and approximate position to find them."

He proceeded to enter *Ciao Bella* and Key West. Immediately up popped a little pink boat shape on a map with the last reported coordinates about six hours ago.

"You see even my doodle could have done that" he chuckled. "Nice work, *Dijon*," who looked up, sniffed and put his head back down.

"Can he show me on a local chart where that is and what is the chance we could take a run out there?"

Lee pulled up his charting software and pointed to a spot about thirty miles up the Overseas Highway off of Big Torch Key.

"He seems to be anchored outside the reef but it would be faster if you drove. You could get a skiff at Dolphin Marina on Little Torch and get pretty close to him."

"This is awesome Lee. Thanks and please give *Dijon* an extra bowl of croquettes from me."

"Wait Finn, what is this all about?"

I shouted back, "Talk to me in a couple of days and I will fill you in, but now I'm on a deadline."

I ran back to the car, grabbing Matt as he was picking up two coffees and a Sunrise sandwich at the White Tarpon.

We arrived at Little Torch Key in less that forty-five minutes and pulled into the Dolphin Marina. It was quiet and we were able to get a small Boston Whaler usually used for fishing the flats. With a couple of poles, some bait and two Tilley hats, we looked like tourists floating around looking for fish to jump into the boat.

Our 140 horsepower Yamaha fired up and we took off looking for the GPS coordinates Lee gave us. After about forty-five minutes of wandering around, we caught site of *Ciao Bella* anchored out.

Rather than simply charging up and asking for a cup of hostage, we cruised toward a couple of mangrove islands not far from the sand flats inside the reef. They probably had us in sight using binoculars but we looked like a dozen other skiffs from rental agencies, a sunburned tourist and a tanned skipper casting for bonefish.

As I stood in the stern of the boat with my face covered by my floppy hat, neck wrap and sunglasses, I figured I was well disguised. Matt was casting, badly I might add, in the direction of the *Ciao Bella* so he could observe the activity on the boat. As a preliminary recon, we could see one guard on the bow and another on the upper deck.

Suddenly, a figured emerged from the main cabin in a bikini and I would have known that ass anywhere. Even from a hundred and fifty yards. Courtney climbed to the upper deck, then stretched out to work on her tan. She did not seem the least bit self-conscious and the guards were more interested in admiring her body than guarding it.

What the hell was going on?

CHAPTER THIRTEEN

I WAS HAVING FANTASIES about rescuing her and here she was at worst a *bird in a gilded cage.* I had been running around for almost three days trying to figure out how to save she and her father from a suspected Nicaraguan drug dealer. Now I find her tanning on the yacht like she owns it.

As a whole new set of thoughts began running through my mind, Ortega appeared on deck. He came out of the salon on the same deck as Courtney, walked over to her, bent down and kissed her. This was getting very strange, three days ago he shoots her father and today he is kissing her.

I figured the Stockholm syndrome took longer than that to kick in so I was not looking at Patty Hearst but rather a co-conspirator. *But to what?*

Matt and I continued fishing for the next hour unproductively but for appearances then headed back to the Marina.

As we packed up and headed back to Key West, my phone rang from a number I did not recognize, nor did my phone give me a clue.

"Hey asshole, have you found him?"

"Found who?"

"Don't be a smart ass, Pilar."

"Who is this?"

"The guy holding your ex and her dear daddy, dumb fuck."

"I'm sorry but you must have the wrong number." I hung up.

He called back but I ignored the call.

I needed time to think and I figured after the lip-lock on the back of Ortega's boat I saw, Courtney was safe. So what the fuck was going on? *I was starting to get a bad feeling.*

In the last seventy-two hours, I have gone from being simply a divorced, disgraced cop who married into Key West royalty to being hired by a drug smuggler to rescue a treasure hunter and having pissed off a different drug smuggler with ties to the Russian Mafia.

I was now in the middle of this from both sides. What more could possibly go wrong I asked myself? *Little did I know... .*

We got back to my house just before the seventy-two hour deadline and as the next call from Ortega came through.

"Hang up on me again asshole and she's dead," he sputtered.

"Fuck you." I hung up. Knowing he wouldn't kill her helped.

He called back and I said, "Listen asshole, I seem to be your only hope of getting your money and finding Daniels so quit jerking me around. Put her on the phone."

After a long pause, Courtney came on and said, "Finn, quit pissing this guy off or I am fucked." I expect from her perspective that was a threat but what I wanted to say was, *I'm sure you would enjoy it.*

Not wanting to let her know what I knew about her lip-lock, I simply said, "Courtney, are you and Roger okay?" The concerned ex in me pretending to show up in the event that Ortega was listening.

"Of course we are not okay, you idiot. Have you found Daniels yet?

A plan had been forming in my head on the drive back to Key West from the Dolphin Marina and I decided to bait the trap.

"Courtney, Ortega needs to understand that Daniels is in the wind. He disappeared and it looks like I am not the only one looking for him. Someone broke into his house before I had a chance to get there and tore it apart. Ortega is a nasty piece of work who seems to be in a battle for control of the drug trade in South Florida. I don't know what you or your father did to piss him off but it might have something to do with Niko Cross."

She asked, "What are you talking about? What has Cross to do with Ortega?"

"Look, as I have been digging into this, it looks like Cross has been smuggling drugs into Florida and laundering the proceeds through a local Russian gang. I think Ortega is a rival for the Florida trade. One of the bodies that showed up here looks to be one of his men. After that someone killed a Russian guy and it may have been Ortega who did it."

Courtney paused and her response was interesting, "Finn, you and your conspiracy theories. Dad borrowed money to complete a hotel project on the north side of the island from Ortega. Ortega wants it back but Daniels seems to have taken off with the money, simple as that. Find Daniels, find the money, return it to Ortega, and we get released. Can you do that?"

Ortega came back on the line and shouted "Finn, quit dicking around, find Daniels and get me my money. You have one more day to find him or I start using your pretty ladies fingers and toes for fish bait," and he hung up. Okay, So I had bought more time.

~ ~ ~

I was beginning to think I was being played. Suppose this kidnapping was in reality a ploy to get me to look for Daniels. If Roger is in fact partnering with Ortega in the drug and laundering business, maybe it is not money that they are after but to find Daniels because he knows something. Ortega and Linebush have used me to find him and I have left a trail a mile wide pointing to me searching for him. They kill him and point the finger at me. They get back at me for putting Wade in prison and they solve a problem all at the same time."

You know what they say. "If you're playing poker and you look around the table to find the patsy and you can't spot him, it's you. "

This was not looking good and it looked like I might need to actually find Daniels.

Before I did anything I needed sleep. Mental processes degrade with lack of sleep and I had a feeling mine was running on at best fifty percent. But before I slept, I needed to do two things: feed and walk Crutch; and second, write down everything I knew so I can share it with my new attorney.

I called Stacy at the Stock Island Marina and asked her if she would like to have dinner. I explained that I had an ulterior motive as I wanted to hire her as my attorney and while she sounded disappointed, she agreed to meet at eight o'clock at Martin's.

I spent the next two hours taking care of Crutch and writing -OK - typing a ten-page summary of the events of the last three days as well. I could have just emailed it to her but they can be subpoenaed and retrieved. I am pretty sure I didn't want my little *enhanced interrogation* of Peter Cross to end up in court. My dark side is buried deep from my time in Iraq but it is there. I also wanted her to have the original tape of Peter and Eddie in the event that I was ever pressured to return it.

Matt and I discussed plans for the evening and he agreed it was probably a good idea to get the tape into the hands of a lawyer. I said I hoped the lawyer would have more than the tape in her hands and told him about Stacy. He decided to head over to the Green Parrot to hear the band and maybe meet a lawyer as well so we agreed to meet up again at eight o'clock the next morning for breakfast at La Creperie on Petronia and parted company.

I was still able to catch a quick nap and a shower before heading out to Martin's, which is only a few blocks from my place. Martin's is a great little place with the best happy hour on the island. Run by two German brothers, it is my go-to place for a first date dinner. I have only been twice for dinner, so as you may surmise, not a lot of first dates.

Even though Stacy sounded a bit disappointed that my invitation for dinner was for business, she dressed like it was a first date. Wow would not cover it. Her dress was a form-fitting Bougainvillea print cut low and was slit from her ankle to her navel. Well almost. Believe me when I say, her form fit the dress perfectly. She had her hair loose and settled on one side of her neck as she sat at the bar with a Key West Sunset Martini and every straight guy in the place admiring her.

I put on my best saunter and strolled up to the bar. Ernie the bartender - yes, I know most of the bartenders in town - asked me what would I like and I said, "Same as the lady." She turned as I sat down beside her.

"This seat taken?" I asked as I turned to look at her.

She smiled and said, "Of all the gin joints, in all the towns, in all the world, you walk into mine."

Who can't help but love a beautiful woman who can quote from Casablanca?

I laughed and replied, "Mademoiselle, I sinc zis is zuh beginning of a beautiful friendship." in a bad French accent. She chuckled

I held out a dollar and said, "I would like to hire you as my lawyer."

She paused, accepted the bill and remarked, "I have a feeling a lot of the girls you meet accept singles." *This girl was funny.*

"Ok, consider it a retainer."

"Fine," she smiled. "But you can expect your hourly rate to be stiff."

I choked on my drink.

To say that we had a fun evening was an understatement. Given all that I was dealing with, it was good to laugh for a couple of hours but as it got late, the last few days caught up to me and I need to wrap things up.

"Stacy, this has been fun but I need to cover a couple of things and call it a night."

"What do you want to cover?" She grinned.

How I wanted to follow that up and make a night of it but I needed sleep. I ignored her suggestive comment and said two things. "A follow up dinner in the very near term, and I need you to hold a package for me." I paused for a second. "Let me rephrase that. I have some documents and a recording that I would like you to keep in a safe place in the event that something happens to me."

Her expression became serious and she said, "What do you mean, something happens to you?"

"Stacy, for the last few days I have been working a case and have stirred up a bit of a shit storm. This package has a statement and a thumb drive with a video. The statement outlines what I know and what I suspect. The video is interesting viewing. If something happens to me, give it to my old partner on the Key West PD, Jeff Sessions, and he will know what to do with it. I hope to get it all resolved in the next twenty-four hours. Just keep it safe."

Her concern was visible but she nodded her head and agreed.

With that I paid the check and we headed out the door. I had Ernie call her a cab and we waited on the curb as one approached.

I asked, "So are we on for a second business meeting?"

To which she replied, "You know how to whistle, don't you Finn? You just put your lips together and ... blow." Then she kissed me, jumped in the cab and drove down the street.

I stood on the sidewalk in awe. *Where has this girl been all my life?*

As I walked along Duval with two Key West Sunset martinis, a great bottle of Opus and a Yellowtail Snapper stuffed with lobster under my belt, echoes of the evening with Stacy bounced around in my head.

Turning down Catherine I failed to register the parked van nor did I see the guy with the Taser until after I was hit in the back and fell to the ground twitching like I was having a seizure. Someone taped my hands behind my back and put duct tape over my mouth. All I saw was pavement, the sidewall of a tire and a head with a distorted face in a stocking mask just before the black hood went over my head.

CHAPTER FOURTEEN

WE BOUNCED ALONG city streets and it reminded me to write my city commissioner about fixing the potholes. As we drove, I was able to track our progress out of town. Bumpy along Whitehead hitting my favorite pothole to avoid in front of the Elks Club, right turn up Truman, street repair bumps up to North Roosevelt then new pavement until we crossed Cow Key bridge then on to U.S. 1.

Then I started counting.

About sixty seconds later we were turning off the main highway and heading right toward the fishing harbor on Stock Island. The van stopped and the side door slid open. I was going to ask if they could stop and pick up a sandwich at Hogfish but with the tape I could only mumble.

The son of a bitch in the mask hit me again with the Taser. When I get out of this I am going to share the experience with him a time or three.

We must have been in a private area near the boats because they dragged me between them down a dock and dumped me onto the deck of a boat. The engines fired up sounding like a big pair of twins, lines were cast off and we idled out of the harbor. So much for tracking where we were headed.

Once out of the harbor and through the no wake zone, the boat was up on plane and doing about twenty-five knots. I felt like it was going north but it was hard to tell. I figured about now Matt would begin to wonder if I was gone for the night but given my comments about Stacy, he would think I would be gone in a good way. He might have met a lawyer as well so I could expect no help there.

The boat began to slow and after a few minutes at idle the engines quit and an anchor dropped over the side. I expected the fun was about to start.

A voice I recognized said, "So were is the video asshole?"

"What video is that?" I mumbled behind the tape and he replied with the Taser then he tore off the tape.

"Motherfucker!" I blurted when I could speak again. "Go fuck yourself!" I almost said Georgi but figured if he didn't know I recognized him it might be an advantage.

"Don't give me any of your wise ass bullshit Finn. We searched your house and we have your phone but the copy is gone. Where the fuck is the video?" and he hit me with the Taser again.

Now one of the things that many people are not aware of, is that during the course of EOD training, we go though a lot of the same training as Navy SEALs including a program called S.E.A.R. meaning Survival, Evasion, Resistance and Escape. I had a feeling Resistance and Escape were going to be more of a priority at this point.

One of the lessons I learned during my special forces training is, *Pain is only fear leaving he body.* At this point I had a lot of fear leaving my body but I also knew that so far no permanent damage had been done. I also think the recording was what they wanted before they would kill me. I had no doubt Georgi would have no problem with that part but his partner might be a little skittish.

"Listen asshole, I don't know who you are but I DON'T HAVE ANY RECORDING, video or otherwise!"

At this point things got a little more serious. "Finn, I know you have it and I want it back," said Eddie.

I made a mental note to make sure he no longer had authorization and access to my investment accounts.

"What's the matter Eddie? Your fuck buddy meal

ticket a little nervous about his peter being shown butt-diving on You Tube in living color? " I can be a little colorful at times.

"Taze this fucker again" and more fear began leaving my body.

I was lying on the deck of the boat with my hands and feet bound with duck tape and a black hood over my head. It reminded me of the Second Phase of BUD/S. I knew if I could get over the side I could at least have a fighting chance in the water.

I sat up and leaned against the stern of the deck. I knew that if this kept up, I could have a problem as each time the Taser is used, my heart was getting closer to V-Fib.

"Get back down on the deck," growled Georgi but as a swell raised the stern of the boat, I launched myself back Key Westward over the twin engines into the water.

The warm water was shallow but deep enough to let me dive to about ten feet. It would be hard so see for a few seconds until they got a light out. Again I fell back on my EOD training and first got my hands under my hips and my legs through my hands. I tore the bag from my head and the tape from my ankles. I could swim about fifty yards with my hands bound before I had to come up for air but in what direction?

I did a slow circle and found the boat about twenty feet away. I swam toward it to get to the bow and came up below the anchor line, hoping it was a place they were not looking.

A quick look and I could see a mangrove island about fifty yards away. I could hear Eddie squealing from the stern, "Go get him, go get him, GO GET HIM!" as Georgi dove off the back.

Great, I thought as I dove down toward the anchor. If I can cut the tape off my wrists with the anchor chain, at least I can swim. I didn't know how good Georgi was at swimming but I'll bet his hand-to-hand combat skills were better than mine. Spetsnaz are world-class soldiers but primarily land-based trained. I should have an advantage in the water. It was time for evasion.

I cut the tape on my wrists and looked around to see if I could spot Georgi. While the water was clear, it was dark and I couldn't see him. I popped to the surface, looked around and oxygenated for a few seconds. Assuming Georgi followed his own preference, he would think I would head for the island as he would have, so I dove deeper and farther away from it. The water in the area is at most thirty to forty feet deep. If I could stay hidden for at least ten minutes, they would probably begin to circle the boat to search for me.

Most people don't know it, but the deeper you dive, the longer you can swim underwater due to the pressure on your lungs. I could do about fifty yards at ten feet so I tried twenty feet and figured I would be out of range of them at about two hundred yards. I dumped my deck shoes and a really nice two hundred dollar Robert Graham shirt that I had worn to dinner but kept on my Arcteryx shorts.

Eddie was going to owe me after this. Still no sign of Georgi.

I came up for air a second time and could see in the distance Eddie pulling up the anchor. Still no sign of Georgi. I dove down again but this time I swam at ninety degrees to my last direction. No point in leaving a trail of disturbed water when I come up to breathe.

Where was that fucker, Georgi? I dove again and spotted him about twenty yards back, his dive light searching for me and he was between me and the boat. Fuck this guy is good.

Time for Plan B.

He did not seem to be gaining on me and I was just out of range of his light but he was searching in the right neighborhood.

I went up for air and dove toward the island. If I could circle around out of his range and get to the boat, I felt sure I could overpower Eddie and leave Georgi behind.

Good plan right?

All was going well as I approached the boat until Georgi spotted me and figured out what I was doing. Now it was a race.

I had to beat him to the boat before he could shout a warning to Eddie.

Time for Plan C.

I took a last breath and dove to about ten feet coming up on the port side away from Georgi. Eddie was leaning over the stern swim platform ready to hook me with a gaff like a marlin on a stick. I pulled myself up on the port side and he turned with his eyes full of hate. He lunged at me with the gaff and missed. I figured I had about ten seconds before this became a two against one fight once Georgi was back on board.

No pain no gain, so I feinted toward the starboard side of the boat and dove for the gaff as Eddie lunged again. The tip caught me on my right arm but I was able to push it back into Eddie. He hooked his foot on a loose line and flipped backwards over the side just as Georgi climbed onto the swim platform with a dive knife in his hand. And me with a gaff hooked in my arm. "Now you are on my turf, Finn," he growled.

CHAPTER FIFTEEN

KNIVES ARE A REAL TERROR especially in the hands of an expert. I needed the gaff out of my arm and available to keep him at a distance, at least to assess the damage from the gaff. This was going to hurt. Luckily the gaff was not barbed, so a quick pull and it slid out of my arm and I swung it forward toward Georgi.

He stepped back and laughed. "You're dead, motherfucker," and came in at me swinging the knife back and forth close to his body before striking out.

As I arched my stomach back from his right arm I caught his wrist with my right hand and twisted it past me with the knife now on my right. My left arm pushed his elbow in toward him and I pulled his wrist back and up. This twisting forced him to drop the knife as I stepped behind him. I then pushed him over the side of the boat.

I swung toward the pilot seat and fired the engines. The boat had drifted close to the mangrove island so I hit the throttles to get it a mile or so from the island, leaving Eddie and Georgi behind. I first checked the GPS to mark the position of the island then searched around for a first aid kit to deal with my arm. I spent the next twenty minutes or so wrapping my arm, cleaning up the blood scattered on the boat and wiping it down for fingerprints.

I headed south and west toward Southernmost Point, then radioed a distress call using my *best Russian, bad English, accent* giving an estimate of the location of the island saying I had seen a flare in the area. I let the boat drift and swam over to South Beach and walked home. So much for a restful night.

~ ~ ~

I passed out and woke to someone banging on my door at eight fifteen a.m. Nothing like a restful two hours sleep. My arm hurt like hell but I put on a long sleeved shirt and stumbled to the door expecting it was Matt because I was late for breakfast.

After all I had been through, I figure it was prudent to look out the peephole before opening the door. That makes a lot of sense especially when you see your ex-wife with a gun pointed at her head standing outside. For a split second I thought I should just ignore the whole thing and go back to bed but being the chivalrous guy that I am, I opened the door.

Standing on the porch was Courtney looking a bit ragged with Ortega standing behind her.

"Finn, please step aside and let us in. This beast will kill me if you don't," she whimpered.

Again I paused. I had considered killing her myself in the past but my better angels had triumphed. Given that I knew she and the *beast* had been making whoopee on the deck of his yacht just yesterday, I figured this was a ploy unless something had changed since then. I doubted he would kill her. I also didn't want them to know I had seen them so I let them into the house.

Ortega looked around and said, "I almost said if you don't sit down I will shoot her in the head and it will mess up your décor but now that I see it, it would probably be an improvement." He laughed.

"Ortega I appreciate the decorating feedback but why are you here and what the fuck do you want?"

"Finn, Finn, Finn," he began. "I had hoped that the lives of your ex-wife and her father would have been enough incentive to get you focused on finding Daniels and my money. It appears I was wrong."

I needed to get this discussion moving along to try and learn what I could. "Look Ortega, in the last three days I have been kidnapped, run over by a pickup and shot at by a Russian sniper. I don't know what you have me involved in but I have not been sipping margaritas and getting a mani/pedi. You need to tell me what is going on here or I cannot get anything more done."

Ortega seemed surprised.

I did not share that I had seen him playing *hide the sausage* with my ex-wife or at least *sucking face.* I have a vivid imagination about the *hide the sausage* part and didn't what to go there.

"WHAT THE FUCK is this all about?" I shouted.

Ortega paused and seemed to reflect for a few seconds. He turned and pointed to the sofa. "Sit down. Let me tell you a hypothetical story."

I knew I was going to have to read between the lines.

"Four years ago, Linebush approached me about lending him money for his construction bonds through my offshore company in the Caymans. His business had grown to the point that he could no longer fund them himself. He offered to repay me from an account he had offshore. It seemed like a good business model. I had a significant amount of cash from my other businesses that I needed to move offshore as well. I made a nice neat twenty percent on the loans to Linebush. He in turn would take my cash *(my thought bubble - drug money)* and export it into my account and he would take twenty percent for his trouble. Everybody wins right?"

"Ok, I'm following the story so far."

"This arrangement worked well until you stepped in and arrested Wade. Wade took care of investing some of the *loans* into projects he was involved in and ended up losing a significant amount."

"How much is a significant amount?" I asked.

Ortega said, "Let's just say it was north of twenty-five million."

Square Grouper

I choked.

"As I'm sure you can appreciate," he continued, "I was concerned, because now Linebush was having trouble with his bonding and began using MY local cash to cover himself. Daniels figured out something was wrong. With Eddie now handling the payments from the investment accounts, it seemed that money was showing up and disappearing from company accounts. Two weeks ago Daniels confronted Eddie. Eddie went to Linebush who called me in a panic. Linebush went to find Daniels and convince him to get on board until this could be straightened out but Daniels took off with his family. "

"So why pick me?"

"Courtney suggested we get you on the trail of Daniels but she knew you would be a hard sell; hence, the *kidnapping* to get your cooperation."

It was now clear that I had been played. Courtney still had me thinking with the little head but pieces of this still do not hang together. Why was Cross involved and why was he trying to kill me? Was Wade really guilty or had Eddie set him up?

"Ok I get the basics of this but what has Cross got to do with any of it?" I posed.

"How the fuck should I know. You'll have to ask him."

Yea, that was really going to happen.

As I sat thinking about this I saw Matt, slowly open the door to the house and pointed my H&K at Ortega.

"Drop the gun fucker, or I will put a hole in your gut and through your spine. Then I will watch you bleed out. Sorry, Finn but it will mess up your carpet."

Everybody seemed to be concerned about my décor. I may have to begin paying more attention to it. "I have been meaning to change the rug anyway so feel free to pop him."

I don't like being played.

110

Ortega kept his gun pointed at Courtney's head and said, "I don't know who you are, but I am going to count to three and kill the girl."

"One, two..." I had stood up when Matt came in and I reached over and yanked the gun out of Ortega's hand.

"Ortega, you are such a dumb fuck. The least you can do is take the safety off before you threaten someone."

Matt laughed and said, "Finn, I thought you would just let him do it. She has been such a bitch and it would cut down on your alimony payments."

As tempting as this might be after her casting me aside, not to mention taking up with this bozo I could only say, "How would I explain it to the kids?"

Courtney about choked when I said that, and sputtered, "What kids?"

"Oh come on sweetie, our beautiful twins, Dublin and Bell. Short for Belfast," I looked over at Ortega as way of explanation. I figured if I was making it up as I went along, I might as well stick with the Irish theme.

Ortega and Courtney both looked flustered and it was hard to tell if it was the fact that I might know they were playing pickle poker or that we had kids. We didn't but it would be fun to watch them try to sort it out.

I said to Matt, "It's okay Matt to put down the gun. Ortega has been explaining to me the background to this whole thing. It seems they were just using me to find Daniels and save their asses from some crazy money-laundering scheme they have going. I could give a shit what happens to them so let them go and we can go get one of Cindy's Bloody Marys."

Courtney looked at me and started to plead, "Please Finn we still need your help. If Daniels talks to the feds then we could all go to jail. You have to help us."

I looked at Matt then said, "Ok, let me put this into simple English so even Ortega here can understand it."

I spoke painfully slow to make the point. "You played me to get me involved and I have been shot at, run down and kidnapped *for real*. Ortega probably killed a Russian working for Cross who now thinks I am working for Ortega. All this to track down and do who knows what to Daniels and potentially try to pin it on me. Did I miss anything?"

Courtney looked at me with steel in her eyes and said, "You always were an asshole Finn and a shitty lay as well. Fuck you."

"Funny thing about that. Peter told me you were so bad it turned him gay." The shitty lay part did hurt so my retort felt good.

She came after me with claws out and only missed when Matt grabbed her from behind. "You haven't heard the last of this Finn," she said and stormed out with Ortega in tow.

I thanked Matt for his help and said, "I have a feeling that is the first honest statement she made all day."

He replied, "I don't know, some of the girls in San Diego said you were a shitty lay as well, but I tried to make up for it with them". As we laughed and relaxed, little did we know what was to come and from what direction.

~ ~ ~

At this point I was ready to get on with my life until Matt reminded me that Cross still thinks I work for Ortega. I doubted if Peter had told him about our adventure at Eddie's place or of the recording I shot. Having said that, I couldn't be sure. Peter was also unlikely to discuss the supposed drug deal that Matt aka Mr. Johnson was involved in after that evening either.

Nor would they have any idea regarding the little raid on the cigarette boat. All in all, it was probably not going to be a big problem for Cross to let it all go. Little did I know there was someone stirring this particular pot to a boil.

~ ~ ~

Eddie was a little more problematic. He knew I had

the recording but had no real way of getting it. He had tried once to get it and involved Cross through Georgi. I had pulled his authority on my accounts but that was small potatoes for him.

I did have five people really pissed off with me though: Courtney, Eddie, Peter, Georgi and Leslie. Six if you count Squeaky.

I didn't.

What was interesting was that Courtney was the common thread. She had introduced me to Eddie many years ago as someone who handled her investments. She had married Peter for whatever reason and Eddie was Peter's gay lover. Even Courtney's brother Wade was involved as Eddie's former business partner.

Georgi and Leslie came with Peter as security and even Squeaky worked for Linebush and now for Cross. It seemed like I needed to figure out why Peter and Courtney got married. It was time for a visit to Cross Senior.

CHAPTER SIXTEEN

OLD MAN CROSS was the one player in the game that I had never met, so I figured now was as good a time as ever. I did however wonder if he would he be willing to do it. The only possible leverage I had was the video of his son and Eddie dressed only in a lime green tutu *doing a pole dance*. Maybe a still picture of that with Peter's face blurred would be enough to get his attention.

I went to my computer and pulled a still off the video and did a quick search for Cross's email address. It was easy enough to find given his public persona as a generous local philanthropist. After sending a quick email, I took a quick shower and fed Crutch. We then headed to Southernmost Café for some breakfast and one of Cindy's Bloody Marys.

Once back at the house, I checked my email and found that someone from Cross's office had responded with an invitation to meet him for lunch at Latitudes. Now Latitudes is one of my favorite restaurants on The Rock even if it is not actually on the island, but on Sunset Key. A twenty-passenger launch makes regular runs from the Westin Pier to Sunset Key for patrons with reservations at Latitudes as well as island residents and guests. Matt and I headed into town and toward the pier. The walk was good to get the kinks out but my lack of sleep was going to catch up with me at some point.

We picked up the shuttle launch, the water in the channel was calm, and the boat traffic minimal. We were docked at the pier on the far side of the island in about ten minutes.

As we walked up the wooden pier toward the entrance

to the restaurant, I could see Georgi standing by the door. He looked like he was ready to pounce as we walked up.

"Good Morning Georgi," I said, "You look like you had a rough night. You should get more rest."

As he took a step toward me I smiled, "I am sure Mr. Cross would love to know more about your adventures with Eddie last evening" I paused, "and why." He said nothing.

"You can get the door for us, thanks."

No, he didn't get the door.

Just past the bar, I could see a gentleman wearing a loud island shirt, white linen pants and a Greek ship captain's hat sitting on the patio with a glass of wine and an unlit cigar. His hair was steel gray and his face lined from the sun but he looked fit and rugged.

As I walked up I suggested, "Mr. Cross I presume?"

"Ah Mr. Pilar, it is with distinct ... reservations that we meet," he replied. "And who is your friend?"

"This is Matt, a friend and insurance agent."

Cross laughed. "Georgi thought he was a body guard."

I laughed, "Does he look like a body guard?"

"Mr. Pilar, what can I do for you?" Right to the point.

The waiter came by so we paused and took a few minutes to order lunch and a bottle of Sonoma-Cutrer.

"Mr. Cross ..." I began.

"Please Finn, call me Niko," he said.

We spent some time on pleasantries such as the beauty of Sunset Key and then I got back to the point. "Alright, Niko, over the last few days I have gotten caught up in some sort of dispute that seems to involve you at a peripheral level."

"Go on," he said.

"It seems that a colleague of Roger Linebush thinks I can help him with a problem and asked me to look around for one of Mr. Linebush's employees. As I proceeded with my enquiries, your son Peter came to my attention and to my surprise I discovered he was married to my ex-wife Courtney."

"Yes, and this was a surprise to you?"

"As a matter of fact, it was quite a surprise. As small a town as this is, we have moved in different circles since our divorce."

"We are very happy to have such a beautiful girl as part of our family, Finn," Cross said. "I am proud of my son for such a catch.

Peter is my only son and has the responsibility to carry on the family name."

Given Courtney's medical history, it would seem that Niko was in for at least one surprise at some point.

"Niko, I have also during the course of my enquiries become aware of Peter's other *special friendships*."

"Mr. Pilar, I am not sure what you are implying."

Our food arrived and it looked fantastic. The lobster roll was set on a bed of lettuce and the fries looked fresh and hot. I wondered if I would get to eat them. The wine had a sheen of moisture on the glass and looked crisp and cold.

"Niko, let me be blunt, Peter is a flamer. He's light in the loafers, he likes to screw men."

To my surprise, this did not seem to bother Cross at all.

"Finn, I am not the least bit interested in your investigations nor your assumptions. Peter understands his responsibilities to the family and what he does in his spare time is none of my affair."

He continued, "I agreed to meet with you because you were at one time married to Courtney and I have great regard for her. Not because of some silly picture you sent."

You could have knocked me over with one of the fries I was salivating over. I took a slug of wine knowing I should be savoring it but I needed a real drink. *There went my leverage - at least most of it.*

"So let me get this straight, *again pun intended,* you had your son marry Courtney even knowing he was gay so he could give you an heir?"

"Mr. Pilar," he said, "my reasons are none of you affair." We were no longer on a first name basis.

"Please, finish your lunch which is on me and I will have Georgi escort you back to town." With that, he got up and walked out of the restaurant.

Matt and I looked at each other and had one of those WTF moments.

Given that Cross was paying for lunch, Matt and I decided to finish our food and the wine. It was time to regroup. If Courtney wasn't a *beard* for Peter, why was she married to him? Peter was unlikely to be fucking her, as he was bare backing Eddie and she would not be interested in risking another STD. It's not out of the question but seemed unlikely.

She knows she can't have kids after she had a backstreet abortion that was botched by a drunken veterinarian. She didn't play football in high school, but she played in every position for the team.

At the same time, Niko knows about Peter, yet seems to think she is going to deliver an heir so ...

"I'm an idiot!" I exclaimed.

"What?" said Matt.

"Courtney isn't a beard for Peter, she is a beard for Niko. He is the one who is screwing her. Peter married her so Niko has lots of opportunity and when she gets pregnant, everyone will think it's Peter's."

"Now that is really weird, dude. Assuming it's true and given that she knows she can't get pregnant, it begs the question, why is she doing it?" asked Matt.

Why indeed?

"We know Niko imports drugs given that he was interested in doing a deal with me as disgruntled ex-cop. We have to assume Georgi told him about it. He didn't mention it to us. so why?"

"Probably didn't want to confirm to us that he knew," surmised Matt.

"The question becomes, who is playing who here? Is Courtney playing Niko, or is Niko playing Courtney, both trying to control the drug trade."

I thought out loud, "and where does Eddie fit in all this, if at all?"

My head was beginning to feel the wine and lack of sleep. I needed a break. We ambled down to the dock with Georgi in tow and caught the next launch back to town. Matt wanted to make some calls to free up the next few days to stay in Key West and I headed home for a few hours sleep.

Crutch greeted me at the door with his usual enthusiasm. He opened one eye, thumped his tail and went back to sleep. I crashed. When I awoke, Matt was dozing on the sofa and the band at La Te Da was in full swing. It was nine p.m. and I had slept for almost seven hours.

Crutch began his *I am hungry routine*, looking pitiful and whining so I prepped his food and water and fed him. I knew it was going to be walk time immediately afterwards so I jumped into the shower then grabbed some clean shorts and a OneBlood t-shirt.

I should explain that the Red Cross gives every blood donor a gift when they donate. I usually opt for the t-shirts that say OneBlood on the back and have a funky Key West local artist silkscreen on the front. Did I mention I was cheap?

As I got Crutch onto his leash, Matt stirred on the sofa.

"The bathroom is yours dude, I need to take Crutch for

his evening stroll."

"Got it," he replied.

Crutch and I took our usual route up Catherine to Simonton, along Simonton to Truman and down Truman to Duval and the Cigar store. I picked up three Robustos and paid the tourist premium as I had not had a chance to get over to my favorite supplier Miguel at Schooner's. As we walked up Duval toward the beach, a cruiser went by with OJ at the wheel. I waved and he waved back, then turned down Catherine.

As I turned the corner, I could see his cruiser parked in front of my place and wondered what was up. As I entered I could see OJ was chatting with Matt. OJ's partner was standing next to him.

"Hey OJ, what's up?" I said as I grabbed a beer from the fridge.

"Good evening Mr. Pilar."

WTF? Mr. Pilar?

"OJ, what is going on?"

"I am here as a courtesy at the moment to see where you've been this afternoon."

The *Mr. Pilar* gave me a clue that this was not a social call. "What is going on?" I asked.

"We are looking into an incident that took place this afternoon and your name has come up as a person of interest. Again, where were you this afternoon?"

"OJ, if she's attractive then I don't mind being a person of interest. I am single as you know."

"Mr. Pilar, for the third time, where were you this afternoon? If you are not willing to answer a few simple questions, then we will need to detain you and take this discussion down to the station."

"Ok Officer." I was starting to get pissed. As an ex cop I expect a little more respect, especially from my former partner. I also know enough not to answer questions until you have a better idea about what is going on. Then have a lawyer present.

"I'll humor you. I had lunch today at Latitudes then came back to the house and slept until taking Crutch for his nightly stroll."

"And who did you have lunch with?"

"What you want all the details? I arrived by launch for the eleven forty-five seating. I had the lobster roll with fries and two glasses of a very nice 2012 Founders Reserve Legacy Sonoma-Cutrer. The host was picking up the tab."

Now my voice got a little more sarcastic. "The fries were a little salty but that's how I like them. The lobster roll was perfection. The bun was fried in butter to a golden brown and the steamed lobster had a sublime aioli sauce and on a bed of butter lettuce. The wine could have been chilled a little more but the ice bucket helped the second glass. Anything else?"

"You still didn't answer my question. Dave, call it in."

Turning to face me he calmly said, "Mr. Pilar, please turn around and put your hands behind your back."

"OJ what is going on?"

"Please turn around and put your hands behind your back, sir."

I complied and he put cuffs on me.

CHAPTER SEVENTEEN

I GAVE STACY'S NAME to Matt as my attorney and asked him to call her to come down to the station. If OJ was going to be a prick then I wanted her around if for no other reason than she looked great. It also saved me my phone call in case I needed another one.

As we rode down to the station I was trying to figure out what I had done that would warrant OJ being such a prick. Eddie might have logged a complaint about the whole grill-marks-on-the-butt thing but OJ would have just laughed.

I *borrowed* Peter's boat last night but that was after being kidnapped, so that probably wasn't it. Finally breaking into Daniels' house was a possibility but with nothing stolen it's really just a misdemeanor.

I had no clue what they think I had done. They put me in the interview room and cuffed me to the table. I waited, and waited and waited. At least they hadn't taken my shoelaces so I wasn't under arrest.

Finally OJ came in with Detective Donnelly, an old fart of a detective with bad breath and a bad comb over. I think most people would confess just to not be in the same room with him.

"Damn, Donnelly, get a breath mint and consider a *Kojak* hair style will you?"

He looked at me with a dull glazed eye. Yea, he actually had only one eye but the department couldn't let him go because his brother was the mayor.

"Finn, I see you are the same ole smartass."

"No seriously, Donnelly. OJ, give the man a Mentos."

Donnelly tried again. "Finn, right now you are only a

person of interest in an investigation."

"Donnelly, I have absolutely no idea what you are talking about but I would like my lawyer present during any questioning. I believe she is on her way and I will not answer any questions until she arrives." At this point, I shut up.

Donnelly looked a little frustrated but he and OJ left the room. Alone again.

About ten minutes later Stacy came in with a smile on her face. "Finn, you do know how to romance a girl, and the ambiance, wow!"

"I figured a girl loves a call from jail as an ice breaker. I hope I didn't interrupt anything." I was fishing.

"I was actually just waiting for someone to invite me to visit the jail and chat with a dangerous suspect. I only had the one class at law school in criminal law so I figured maybe I would get a chance to learn more."

"You know how to make a guy comfortable with his attorney."

"Don't worry I got a B+." She smiled sweetly.

I laughed and thought she at least looks great even at eleven at night, maybe even better if that is possible. I wondered what she'd look like at eight in the morning. *I was clearly not taking my current predicament seriously enough.*

Donnelly came in and Stacy immediately got out a box of Tic Tacs. She may be new to criminal law but not to Key West detectives.

"Let the games begin," I said.

"Detective, are you charging my client?" Go for the gusto baby.

"Miss, your client is a person of interest in an ongoing investigation."

"If you are not charging him with anything then remove the cuffs and bring him some water. You have had him in here for almost two hours and lack of water and dehydration can be used as a reason for dismissing testimony in a tropical climate."

Wow, she is good for a one B+ class attorney. Donnelly looked flustered and after a second removed the cuffs and went out for water.

"I didn't know you could dismiss testimony for dehydration of the witness."

She smiled, "I don't know either but it sounded good and he didn't call bullshit so why not?"

I laughed. Donnelly came back with water and sat down.

"Finn, your name has come up as a person of interest in ..."

"Donnelly you keep saying that but what is it about? For all I know this is parking violation for my scooter or not cleaning up after Crutch that time when I had no poop bags - you know, the usual crimes in Key West."

"Mr. Pilar," he said indignantly, "We are investigating a suspicious death and your name came up"

Now that got my attention.

"Who died?" I asked.

"I am not at liberty to say but ... "

"Yea, I know, my name came up."

"Where were you from three to nine p.m. today?" he asked.

"You don't have to answer that," said Stacy. *Don't you love this girl?*

"Finn, we can issue a material witness warrant and hold you for as long as necessary to prevent a failure of justice if you refuse to answer some simple questions, so you chose."

Stacy once again jumped in and said, "That presupposes a crime has been committed. Has a crime been committed?" *I really love this girl!*

Donnelly replied, "At this point it is not clear until the ME conducts an autopsy. A call came to us saying that Finn was seen in the area and we found an as yet unidentified body in the vicinity where he was seen."

At this point OJ came in and whispered into Donnelly's ear. Better him than me that close to Donnelly, even with the Tic-Tac's.

"Finn", said Donnelly," it has been determined that a body identified as Roger Linebush as been found off Southernmost Point. A caller reported the body off the point and said they saw you dumping it in the water early this evening."

Oh shit.

"Again I would like to know were you were between three and nine this evening"

"Look Donnelly, you know this is bogus right. Why would I kill Linebush?"

As soon as I said it I knew it sounded stupid. I had put his son in jail, I had divorced his daughter and he got me kicked off the force.

"Forget I said that"

"Can anyone testify to your whereabouts at the time you were seen?"

"How would I know? I was asleep."

"Was anyone with you?"

Stacy looked at me. I think she was interested in this answer.

"How would I know? I was asleep."

"Donnelly," I said, "why don't you ask Matt what time he got back to my place. He can probably tell you that I was home in bed."

Donnelly looked at me with a raised eyebrow.

"No you idiot," I said. I can be endearing like that.

"Not in my bed. He is staying at my place while he's in town and he was asleep on the sofa at the time I woke up."

"We will follow up with him. Do you own a gun?"

"You don't have to answer that," said Stacy.

"You heard her," I said.

"When did you last speak to Linebush?" Donnelly asked.

"You don't have to answer that," countered Stacy.

"You heard her," I said.

"Under what circumstances did you last speak to him?"

"You don't have to answer that," said Stacy.

"You heard her," I repeated.

Donnelly was clearly getting frustrated.

"Look Donnelly, unless you are going to charge me as either a material witness or a suspect, then you need to let me go. I am not going anywhere."

Donnelly rose from the table, paused and said with a smile, "You're right Finn, you aren't going anywhere. We are going to hold you for the next twenty-four hours while we execute a search warrant of your house. Based on that, we will discuss next steps." And with that he walked out.

"This is bullshit, Stacy. Any options?"

Stacy shrugged and said, "They seem to have enough to request a search warrant and I will try to find out what, but you are going to have to cool your heels for at least a little bit. "

She continued thoughtfully, "Let me see what I can find out and I will get back with you. And Finn, try to not piss Donnelly off any more that you already have with that winning personality of yours."

"Thanks for coming Stacy and for the Tic Tacs." She smiled, then laughed and turned to leave. I was really beginning to like that laugh. *Laugh while you can, as you never know when a shit storm is going to land on you.*

~ ~ ~

Now the Monroe County lock up is not a bad place.

Most of the *guests* are tourists sobering up after a hard night partying at Sloppy Joe's or Irish Kevin's. The other cohort is the homeless picked up for drunk and disorderly conduct. Other than poor hygiene and piss-stained clothes, they are pretty much the same. I was not too concerned, as most had no idea that I was an ex-cop so I figured I would continue to catch up on my sleep.

Around five a.m., I awoke with a start to find a homeless guy trying to rummage through my pockets. At least that is what I hoped he was trying to do.

"What the hell are you doing, dude?"

He looked at me with bleary eyes and said, "Jus loging fu cigs, mn."

"Well piss off."

"Fuk u, mn" he mumbled and wandered off. *Ah the joys of the Monroe County Detention Center life.*

At six a.m., they let out the homeless and the tourists began to lawyer up for a quick fine and release. Just another story to tell about their wild time in Key West. It was looking like it was going to be *three hots and a cot* for me until Stacy came to see me. She arrived about twelve thirty and saved me from the County gourmet lunch of Spam on Wonder Bread and a mealy apple.

I think my next case will be an investigation into the meal planning and how much ends up in the Sheriff's hands. Rumor has it that he pays his kids to make the sandwiches and charges the County. Talk about a captive clientele. Clearly three hots is misleading advertising.

Stacy was not her bubbly self and said, "Well I have good news and bad news. Which do you want first?"

Now I hate that phrase but I was starved for both food and news so I played along. "Ok did you bring me food and what's the good news?" I asked.

"No but the good news is I found out why they are holding you. You are the prime suspect in the murder of your ex father-in-law"

"Shit, that's the good news?"

"Yep, the bad news is that during a search of your house they found a gun which they suspect is the weapon used in the shooting. They are examining it for prints and doing a ballistic test on it as we speak."

"OK, well I can explain the weapon. I have an H&K USP 40 I keep in my dresser drawer so that should be no problem. Matt had it last night and probably left it out."

Stacy did not look happy when she said, "the gun they found was in a shed attached to your house and it was a Colt Woodsman 22 that has been recently fired."

Oh shit. What is going on? My flashback was to the previous day when Courtney and Ortega came by the house. The gun Ortega had was the same or similar to the one that he had used on Linebush when we were on the boat, a Colt Woodsman 22.

The problem was, that I had grabbed it from him so my prints would be all over it. *This was looking more and more like a set up.*

CHAPTER EIGHTEEN

DONNELLY WAS SOON GOING to have Motive (ex father-in-law destroys my career), Means (Colt Woodsman 22 found at my house) and Opportunity (no alibi as I was asleep) plus a witness who says he saw me at the scene.

"Stacy, this is going to get worse." And I walked her through the whole sordid story.

After listening patiently through the half hour tale, she said. "You're fucked, Finn."

Nice, what happened to my cheerleader?

"Stacy, that is not helpful. How about a little, "Don't worry Finn we will get you through this together. Or, the two of us can beat this Finn."

Stacy smiled and said, "Finn you need a better lawyer than me to handle this one. My B+ is not going to cut it."

"Stacy, call me a hopeless romantic but I trust you. A B+ is better than at least fifty percent of your class. Besides. I know I'm innocent.

As we paused to reflect on where our attorney-client relationship was going, Donnelly walked in.

"Pilar, you're an asshole but it seems your buddy says you were at the house when the body was dumped. I don't believe him but until I can prove he lied, and I will prove it, all we have is the gun. Even though your prints are on it and we found it at your house, it is not enough to hold you. For all I know, you two are in this together. For now though you are free to go."

I had a bunch of smart ass thoughts about Donnelly, but was mindful of Stacy's suggestion so I simply said, "Donnelly, I am sure that a detective with your skills and ability will find a way to solve this case."

Actually no, what I really said was, "Donnelly, you couldn't find your dick much less solve this case but don't let that stop you from trying ... to find your dick that is." My better angels seldom show up.

Stacy laughed and Donnelly blustered. His face took on the color of the Spam in my discarded lunch sandwich and he looked ready to take a swing at me. Stacy took my arm and stepped between us. This girl has brains and guts not to mention good sense. After what seemed like forever I was able to check out of the Marion County lock up and headed back to my place.

Matt was sitting on the sofa with his feet up on the coffee table, beer in hand.

"Welcome back dude, how was your vacation?"

"Island paradise; private suite, view to die for, five-star dining, room service, and a uniformed staff to handle your every need. Even had a guy offer a massage. All at a price you can't beat."

"Glad you enjoyed it, now what?"

Stacy chimed in with, "Will you two quit with the Abbott and Costello routine. This is not over."

We both stared at her and I said, "You know Abbot and Costello?" *I thought I had died and gone to heaven.* A sexy, smart twenty something woman who knew about great old comedy. "Where did you learn about them?

She said, "Are you kidding?"

Her voice shifted into a spot-on impression of Bud Abbott from Abbott and Costello's hilarious *Who's On First*. "Now on the Saint Louis team they have, Who's on first, What's on second and I Don't Know on third."

I jumped in with my best Lou Costello "That's what I want to find out, I want you to tell me the names of the fellows on the Saint Louis team."

She continued, "that's what I'm telling you, Who's on first, What's on Second, I don't knows is on Third ..."

We all broke up.

Surprise, surprise, Crutch after playing aloof and standoffish for being ignored for the last twenty-four hours while I was on *vacation* seemed to have made his point and came over for a scratch behind his ear. After a quickie, he went over to Stacy and curled up by her. Now that was a first. Usually he would hustle treats from visitors but this was the first time he had ever showed any attraction or affection to one. He had even growled at Courtney when she came over with Ortega. *The dog clearly had good taste.*

I went over to the cooler and took out four beers. I poured one in Crutch's bowl and took the others for the group. Okay for you PETA lovers, Key West canines require special treatment. In the heat of summer, you will often see a dog on a bar stool with a beer in a bowl. It's just for hydration.

I toasted Matt and thanked him for backing me up with an alibi. He just nodded.

We were becoming the Three Musketeers.

"Well it seems to me we have a major set up going on and I am on the receiving end. Who is trying to do this and why? Any ideas?"

Matt chimed in with, "We know that Courtney and Ortega had the gun, at least one like it, two days ago and we know you touched it. We know it was a man who called in the *eyewitness account* of Linebush's body being dumped. Who have you pissed off Finn?"

I thought about it for a second and tried out a theory I had been working on while at County. "Let's assume it is Ortega. He has the gun, he already shot Linebush once and he is probably humping Courtney. If Linebush can't pay him the money he owes him, Ortega kills him and is looking for Courtney to repay him assuming she is now in charge of the family fortune. He then tries to *literally* lay the killing on my doorstep to cover his tracks. He figures I have motive, means and opportunity and was not counting on you to back me up."

Matt seemed to think about this for a bit then jumped in with his own theory. "Lets try this on for size. I'm thinking that planting the gun is the key. Only two people we know of knew about the gun and your prints. Courtney and Ortega. Courtney is sleeping with Ortega and Cross. They are bitter rivals for the drug trade. Courtney takes the gun, shoots her father and plants it on you to get you out of the picture."

"Why would she shoot her father for God's sake?" asked Stacy

"Ok it's not perfect," said Matt "but I agree with Finn and expect Courtney benefits from her father's death in some way. I would be looking into what that might be. What if she gets to take over his businesses in the absence of her brother?"

"Wow man, you are dark," Stacy offered.

I chimed in, "Well think about it. She's appears to be screwing both Ortega and Cross, she is married to Cross's son Peter and she may now be running the Linebush family businesses. Now that is a potential merger made in hell."

As I thought about it, two items came up for me. "Let's assume that you are close. It seems to me that Ortega is at risk. Let's assume that Courtney kills Ortega in a fit of rage for his killing her father. She gets the Linebush businesses; Cross-gets the drug business under his control, I'm out of the way and they sleep happily ever after. I think we are at least fishing in the right pond." I added, "But there are a lot of pieces missing."

"So where do you want to start to get some proof?" asked Stacy.

The more I thought about it the more I thought I needed to talk to Ortega. He would be at risk whether he *or* Courtney killed her father. Also, we needed to find out if Courtney stood to gain from her father's death.

"Stacy, is there any way to determine if Courtney benefits from her father's demise?"

She thought about it for a moment and said, "We could wait for the will to be read but that could take months or even a year. It is possible that the company records have a documented succession plan. Public works projects require a lot of documentation so I am thinking I can get a look at County records to see if any of the bids that Linebush Construction filed have a succession plan provision in them naming Courtney to take over the company in the event of the death of the CEO. There could also be Key Man Insurance in place that is needed for bonding a big project. I can follow up on these two things."

I told you she was a smart girl. "I bet you got at least a B+ in corporate law."

"Actually an A-"

I love this girl. Did I say that out loud yet?

"Ok, Stacy if you can follow up on that, Matt and I will try to find Ortega. Let's try to meet back here for happy hour and compare notes." *Happy hour is a part of any healthy Key West investigation.*

Stacy took off and Matt started checking Marinetraffic.com to find *Ciao Bella*.

After his beer, Crutch needed a stroll to his favorite watering holes. I walked down Duval to South Street and up South to Simonton then back toward Truman. We paused numerous times as Crutch re-marked his territory and sniffed around to check who was scouting his turf.

This gave me more time to ponder the various scenarios we had developed. Stacy was trying to track down motive for Courtney; means was pretty obvious, and opportunity was unclear. Would Courtney really kill her father, I doubted it. She may be a lot of things but I didn't see her capable of murder. And what about Ortega? He potentially stood to get his money back if he could get Linebush to pay up. So where did the money go? Eddie?

Eddie handled at least some of the Linebush accounts specifically Courtney's and Corporate. Millions went through his hands between the corporate projects and potentially the laundering of money from drugs and treasure. Ortega wanted me to find Daniels but why? Who told him it was Daniels who could get it back? What if Eddie had been stealing from Linebush and it was discovered? But how would he get the gun and access to Linebush? Where was Linebush actually killed?

This was getting way too complicated. I needed a plan. Instead I went back the Southernmost Café for a Bloody Mary. After a chat with Cindy and a few tricks from Crutch, we headed home. It was time to rattle some cages.

~ ~ ~

Matt had found the last known position of *Ciao Bella* and it appeared to be heading into the new marina on Stock Island, the one Stacy was helping her father run when she was not being my lawyer. I needed to pay Ortega a visit to see what he knows and perhaps to warn him.

Based on its last position, *Ciao Bella* should be getting into the marina any time now so Matt and I hopped into his car and drove to Stock Island. We arrived in time to see *Ciao Bella* approaching the dock. We decided to wait and see what happened next. We sat in the Shrimp Road Grill in the Marina Village complex and ordered Bud Lights while watching the stern and back decks.

As the boat tied up, an ambulance pulled up to the back deck and we sat stunned as a stretcher was taken on board. A few minutes later a body was off-loaded down the ramp on the side and wheeled into the ambulance. There was no siren and no one appeared to be any hurry so it seemed obvious it was a body not a patient.

But who?

We waited.

We saw no sign of Ortega so I put in a call to OJ. After four rings it went to voicemail.

"OJ, it's Finn. Call me when you get this message. It's urgent."

Matt and I waited for another half hour. It was time to order another beer or head out. As we were paying the tab, a police car pulled into the parking lot and two cops walked over to the ramp. A crewmember came out on the back deck and invited them on board. On the back deck, they were invited to sit down and a minute or so later the Captain and Courtney came out of the salon and sat down with them. From where we were sitting it looked like they were taking statements. What the hell was going on?

I called the news desk of the Key West Citizen and reported a body being taken off the *Ciao Bella* and two police officers interviewing the Captain and Courtney Linebush. I figured let the newspaper do the heavy lifting and keep me out of it. Matt and I paid the bill and left. It was time to get back to the house and see what Stacy had come up with for a motive. It looked like it might be too late to talk to Ortega.

As I hung up the phone and as we were walking out of the Grill, I grabbed Matt's arm. To my true surprise, I saw Ortega walk out of the salon and sit down with the cops. Now we have Courtney married to Peter and Ortega who is screwing Courtney, together on Ortega's yacht after a body of unknown identity has been taken off the boat. We rode back to the house in silence trying to figure out what was going on and to make the pieces of the puzzle fit.

CHAPTER NINETEEN

BACK AT THE COTTAGE, Stacy and Crutch were practicing a new trick. He was attempting a back flip for a treat but with only one front leg he was having a bit of trouble sticking the landing. Seemed a bit cruel to me but he seemed to enjoy working with Stacy as much as I did.

We gave an update of our adventures at the Marina and Stacy listened intently until finally saying, "So who is the body they took away?"

"Now that is the question. Who else could be on the boat? We know Linebush is dead and Ortega is alive."

"Stacy, what did you find out with your research?" Matt asked.

"Well, I started with the company filings and nothing showed up about succession. Because Linebush LLC is private it's hard to get any records, as they don't have to file publically. What I did find is that for public bids on construction projects for the city, you are required to disclose the officers and shareholders of the company. Presumably this is done to show that no public officials stand to benefit as shareholders from a company being selected for a project."

She continued her litany of knowledge, "In the event of the death of a major shareholder, the company is required to disclose within forty-eight hours any change in ownership resulting from the death. Linebush has about twenty-four hours to disclose the change, or funding is withheld until such time as disclosure is made. A fine of twenty-five thousands dollars a day is levied and withheld from future payments for each day disclosure is withheld."

"Anything about ownership," I asked?

"I did discover that Courtney is a twenty-five percent owner of the company and her father owns fifty point one percent and Wade has twenty-four point nine currently held in trust while he is in prison."

"So what happens if Linebush dies?" I asked.

"Well that is where this gets interesting. The shares from old man Linebush are held in a trust with the trust held equally between Courtney and Wade. "

"You're joking! How did you figure that out?"

"It took a bit of digging but I have a contact at the public records office, a guy who had a crush on me in high school."

I could totally get that.

"I told him I was working on a case and needed to see the filings for the roadwork Linebush bid on for the North Roosevelt reconstruction. It showed the structure of the trust and upon the death of Linebush it would result in Courtney taking over the company through the trust."

Damn I thought, that gives us a motive for Courtney but as much as I was pissed with her, I found it hard to believe she would kill her own father.

"Before you celebrate," Stacy said, "there's a wrinkle. The trust controls the shares until the estate is settled and in the interim the trustee votes all the shares."

"Ok so don't keep me in suspense who is the trustee?"

"Drum roll please," said Stacy. "It's Eddie Ransom!"

"You're shitting me," I said.

"Nope he is it, at least until the estate is settled which could be a year or more."

Could Eddie have killed Linebush? With Linebush dead and control of his estate in Eddie's hands at least for a while, Ortega would lose his money-laundering partner unless he went to Eddie. What does that mean with Peter and Eddie already in bed together, so to speak.

Did Cross know about Courtney and Ortega? Cross

and Ortega are already in a blood feud that involved potentially two murders. It was beginning to feel like a simmering feud had come to a boil.

"Well folks, this is getting weirder by the minute. It feels like open warfare between these two families but why involve me?"

"Finn," said Matt, "You may know something about Courtney or the family from your time together that caused them to feel you were a risk. Can you think of anything?"

I decided it was time to share the information about Courtney's inability to have kids. "The only thing I can think of is that I know Courtney cannot have children. I suspect old man Cross is hoping to get his family legacy extended by having her marry Peter, then the old man gets her knocked up. Everyone thinks its Peter's and the legacy is secure. It seems a bit of a stretch but crazier things have happened."

Stacy asked, "Does anyone else know about this?"

"I doubt it, Courtney finally 'fessed up about two years into our marriage when I thought we had been trying to have kids. She refused to see a doctor about it. She got drunk one night and we fought about it. She said that her brother had found her a back street abortionist a few Keys up who botched the job so she couldn't have kids. I suppose Wade knows unless she said she was asking for a friend."

At this point Matt jumped in, "People, this is all just speculation. We need to get some solid evidence or we are just pissing into the wind."

"What do you suggest?" asked Stacy.

"In the SEALs, we were taught that sometimes you need to draw out the enemy so they will reveal their position. It's called the *tethered goat strategy*."

Stacy looked at him with a blank look so he went on.

"The tethered goat is the bait. It was used by primitive tribes to tempt predators, say a lion, to come out of hiding to kill a seemingly vulnerable target, the goat. The villagers then pounced on the lion and killed it."

"Sounds risky to me," she said.

"It is but it often worked in Afghanistan."

"What do you mean by *often worked?*" she asked.

"We would send out a patrol but have snipers watch over the patrol waiting for the enemy to attack. With the right coverage it was a good way to expose the enemy. Having said that occasionally, we would lose a soldier on patrol."

Stacy was a bulldog. "I don't like it when you say *occasionally.*"

"Stacy, in war and frankly in life, *We plan; God laughs.*"

"So who do you have in mind for the goat?" I asked to change the subject.

Matt paused and said, "You are probably not going to like it."

"So try me."

"Courtney."

"You're right, it is a bad idea." My better angels jump in and I am a knight in shining armor defending the damsel in distress. *Naw, I am a guy, still remembering with the little head.*

"Just hear me out," Matt said. "We have two factions fighting it out already, right?"

We shook our heads in agreement.

"Cross doesn't know Courtney can't have kids and probably doesn't know she is sleeping with Ortega. Ortega probably doesn't know Courtney is sleeping with Cross. So she is playing both sides. If they are both in the dark, then both should react, right?"

Again we agreed.

"If only one or the other is in the dark, then that one will probably react and the other will be our suspect."

"At this point, Stacy jumps in and says, "Two questions: How do we get this information to both these guys; and how will we see who reacts."

As usual, she is asking the right questions.

I thought about it for a minute then proposed, "We have a funeral coming up at Saint Paul's Church for old man Linebush in two days. It is going to be a huge event with anybody who is anybody in the city attending. I expect that both Cross and Ortega will be there as will Eddie, Peter and Courtney."

Now I get sinister. "How about I tell Ortega as a word to the wise that Courtney is fucking Cross and thus is very close to his arch rival. If he doesn't react then we know he is in on it somehow. If he does react and charges over to Cross or to Courtney then we know Cross is behind this deal."

Matt says, "Why not go to Cross first?"

"Cross and Linebush have been rivals for years and have found a way to at least get along. Ortega is the new guy in the mix and is making his bones here. I think he is the more likely to react and confront Cross. Cross is a very cool player here and is more likely to get even, not mad. Remember the Russian who was Cross's guy turned up dead first and Cross then killed one of Ortega's men."

"Good point. So what do we do between now and the funeral?"

Stacy ever the bulldog, asked, "So what if neither reacts?"

Ok so no plan is perfect.

"If neither reacts then we will need to throw in the kid issue to see what Cross does."

No plan survives first contact with the enemy; in this case, events.

CHAPTER TWENTY

I DROVE STACY HOME and in my best Boy Scout fashion gave her a peck on the cheek at the door intending to head home. She however, had other plans.

The peck became a deep dive as we stood on the front porch of her town home by the golf course. I had almost forgotten the feel of a woman's touch. Courtney and I had had a vigorous sex life but much of it was like a test to see who could get the other off first. It was more competition than collaboration.

From the start, Stacy was both aggressive and yielding. It was like an Argentinian tango, not a heavy metal mosh pit. We fit together perfectly and it seemed that rather than me leading, it was more like she let me lead but with a firm understanding of what she wanted.

We made it though the door, and about half way to what I suspected was the bedroom but the Persian rug in the living room beckoned and we collapsed on the sofa and rolled down to the floor. I don't remember how we got undressed but we continued our dance. I could not remember ever touching skin so soft and the curve of her breasts was both firm and yielding. She was blessed with a muscle tone ... yada, yada, yada.

Damn that was amazing. We came up for air and I was covered in sweat and completely out of breath. She smiled and kissed me softly on the cheek. She laughed and said, "You seemed to want a peck on the cheek to start so there you go."

I laughed and shared, "I was a Boy Scout after all and in fact an Eagle Scout."

"Then while I can't give you a badge, I could get you

some wine."

She stood up and walked naked, uninhibited and seductively to the fridge, took out a bottle of Rombauer Chardonnay and beckoned me to continue our journey to the bedroom. *How did I ever get this lucky?*

As the night wore on we alternatively sipped, sucked, savored and slept. *Alliteration has its place.*

We semi-awoke around eight and collapsed in each other's arms, me wondering again if this was a dream. For a few moments I just stared at her as she again dozed. The sheets were draped over her hips leaving one arm lying across her belly and her breasts leaning slightly toward me. Her face was smooth and peaceful in sleep and I could not resist leaning toward her and kissing her cheek. She stirred and her eyes fluttered open. Her hand lay near me and she reached down and smiled, "Well aren't you the early riser."

She climbed up above me and gently lowered herself down, her breasts inviting a kiss. Slowly we established a rhythm and as our pace quickened her breath came in short gasps. Soon we were both panting as she rode and I bucked. When we were both spent, she chuckled and said, "I'm glad I hung on for more than eight seconds!"

I broke up. She fell on her side laughing and I said, "Giddy up."

After our morning delight, a quick shower and breakfast, I offered her a lift to the Marina but she said she should not show up with me because she was my lawyer.

We agreed to meet for dinner and I headed home. Crutch needed his walk and Matt was probably wondering if I had been kidnapped again.

I must admit to feeling a little guilty. I am thirty-eight and Stacy is twenty-seven. Not exactly robbing the cradle but going by the old rule of thumb, *half your age plus seven* it's right on the border. Having said that, I could not remember feeling so content even with all the bad stuff that was happening around me.

Crutch actually seemed happy to see me and danced around my feet. Probably just had to eat and pee. Matt had put on coffee and seemed to have stepped out for his AM breakfast burrito. The morning was actually quite cool with a gentle on-shore breeze.

I decided Crutch and I needed a bit of exercise so I grabbed my bike and swim suit then headed for a short ride to loosen things up. Crutched liked to run beside the bike for the first mile or so, then he would ride in the basket. I picked up the pace and we swung up United. He hung in and ran as far as White Street. I stopped at the White Street Pier and poured water in a plastic glass I carry for Crutch. He drank deeply then I carried him in the basket as I rode up Atlantic, over to South Roosevelt and up to the airport. We did a U-turn and rode down and over to Southernmost Beach Café.

Cindy had my Bloody Mary ready in a flash and Crutch started to perform the new trick, the back flip Stacy had been teaching him. Cindy thought it was outstanding except for the landing and gave him an extra treat. He settled down behind the bar and I took off for my morning swim. After about thirty minutes I came back in for my post swim Bloody Mary to find OJ and his partner.

"Sup OJ?" I asked.

"Thought I might find you here, Finn."

"Man needs his exercise" I said sipping my Bloody Mary.

"I can see that. Is that the first or the second?" he said with a bit of judgment attached to it.

"I don't keep track. When did *you* start?

"Just looking out for you man."

"Thanks. So I repeat, Sup?"

"Finn, where were you last night?"

147

Oh shit, now what? I wanted to say, What the fuck business is it of yours? But instead I said, "What the fuck business is it of yours?" I know, not my best moment but I had been up half the night with Stacy and had now downed two Bloody Marys. OJ was surprisingly calm.

"Finn, don't go all *What the fuck business is it of yours?* on me.'"

"We have a second situation we're dealing with. You seem to have shown up in the middle of them both."

"What now OJ?" I said trying to change the subject.

"Where were you last night?" Changing the subject didn't work.

"OJ, I have no comment until you tell me why you want to know."

OJ passed his detectives exam and was waiting for his shield but after eight years as his partner I still think of him as an Officer and I still called him OJ rather than DJ.

"Finn we took a body off a boat moored at Stock Island Marina Village and when we talked to witnesses, your name came up"

Oh Shit, now what?

"When was the body removed?" I asked.

OJ said, " We took the body off the boat around four yesterday afternoon."

"So why do you need to know where I was last night?"

"The office of the deceased was broken into last night and the place was trashed. Someone was looking for something."

"So why come to me? Wait a minute, ... whose office was trashed and for that matter, who is deceased?"

"I am not at liberty to say at this time, so where were you?"

"I was with my attorney," I replied

"And what is his name?" OJ was always a bit of a sexist.

"Her name is Stacy, Stacy Barnett."

OJ stared at me, "You mean Joe Barnett's daughter. She can't be more than nineteen dude!"

"Actually she has been out of law school for a year and is working for her Dad," I replied.

"She can verify this?" he asked then paused, "All night?"

"You'll have to ask her." I said.

He looked at me with a look of both judgment and envy. "Jesus." was all he said.

At this point OJ and his partner, Rex or something like that turned and left, leaving me and Crutch to wonder who the hell had just turned up dead. I had a sinking feeling in my stomach as we rode back to the house. I didn't have to wait long for the answer.

~ ~ ~

At home for a nap after my fun night and I ended up sleeping until one. Matt had come and gone while I slept so I called him on his cell.

"Afternoon sleepy head," he chuckled. "Long night perhaps?"

"I was working on my legal case with my lawyer," I said with mock indignation. "This type of case is complex."

"I'll say dude. The *ins and outs* of this kind of legal work can really run *up* the fees."

"Enough, enough." I begged. "What have you been UP to?"

"Well while you were exploring the legal world, I decided to take another look at the finances of Linebush. I did a little research through my insurance contacts and it turns out that a Key Man policy for ten million dollars was written three years ago on the old man and paid for by Linebush LLC. In the event of Roger's death, the company gets the ten million. This is all in the trust and under Eddie's control until the estate is settled."

"That is great Matt, ten million motives for Eddie by the sounds of it."

"That is the good news, do you want the bad news?"

"No," I said. "Alright give it to me."

"You know the body they took off *Ciao Bella* yesterday? The press reported today that it was the body of a prominent financial planner in the city."

"Oh shit. Not Eddie?" I gasped.

"None other." said Matt.

"How did he die?"

"It appears that he drowned, he was floating in about twenty feet of water with dive gear on and his leg caught in a fishing net of some kind. The body was retrieved by the crew of the *Ciao Bella* off their anchorage near Coupon Bight off Big Pine."

"Son of a bitch, where's the body now?"

"The coroner has the body and they are trying to see if there is anything suspicious."

"Okay, Robo, I need to get Stacy working on the next-in-line for control of the company with Eddie out of the picture. I will talk to you later." And I hung up.

With Eddie out of the equation, it was critical to find out who took over in the event of his death. They were either the killer *or* at risk. With millions on the line, it was clear that someone was very keen to get their hands on the money.

I called Stacy and she was out but her sexy voice mail (ok I was smitten), said she would be back in twenty minutes. I left a message and decided to try to set up a call with Wade. It is not easy to talk to someone in prison, at least by phone. I called OJ and asked him if he was up for a beer. We agreed to meet at Viva Salon on Duval after his shift ended at four p.m. It was time to get him at least part way into the loop.

In the meantime, Stacy called me back. "Afternoon lover,"

she said as an opening. "Did you get a nap? I know you old guys need your beauty sleep."

"Old guy! Wait a minute, I thought it was kids who needed their afternoon naps."

She chuckled and said, "So what's up? Hang on, let me rephrase that. What can I do for you? No, that won't work either. What can I do *to* you? Never mind. Sup?"

Rather than take any more time on sexual innuendo I jumped in with, "The body they took off the Ciao Bella yesterday was Eddie Ransom. It looks like he drowned; may be accidental but still under investigation. Also Matt found out there is a ten million dollar insurance policy on Linebush payable to the company. With Eddie out of the picture who takes over the trust? Also is there a way to see if Eddie was a certified diver, maybe look at the PADI website."

"Ok anything else?"

"Yes, get back to me as quick as you can and can you meet me at Martin's for Happy Hour, then dinner at five-thirty? They have half-price appies and martinis till six."

She chuckled and said, "You really know how to flatter a girl Finn. Should I bring a big purse so we can steal the salt and pepper shakers and martini glasses that come with the senior's dinner special?"

"Are you making fun of my stemware collection?"

I could hear her smile. She whispered, "See you soon, big boy," as she hung up.

Damn this girl is fun.

I took the next couple of hours to put together the information I wanted to share with OJ. It needed to be enough to get him interested but not enough to incriminate me. I hoped to hear from Stacy before I met him but it was a lot to ask of her. As four o'clock approached, I had my ducks in a row and figured it was time to get the law on the case.

CHAPTER TWENTY-ONE

VIVA SALON IS A FUNKY, old Key West bar that had been closed for fifteen years until the building owner found an enterprising young entrepreneur willing to take if on as a project. Patched together on a wing and a prayer, he furnished it with garage sale tables and mismatched chairs, found a popcorn machine and opened with as much beer and liquor as he could get with a thousand bucks of credit.

It has table seating facing Duval Street through large openings where the windows fold back and a large parking lot beside it with tables and chairs. He would often show football games and movies on an inflatable screen in the parking lot. His long-term plan was to invite food trucks to the large parking lot to handle the more refined palate for things other than popcorn. With two-dollar Buds it is usually full.

OJ came in on time for once and we sat in a back corner while I laid out the situation. I shared the original call from Linebush, the visit to the *Ciao Bella* and Ortega's seventy-two hours to find Daniels and the threat and shooting of Roger. My scramble to figure out what was going on, the extended deadline and the further threat of harm to Courtney by Ortega at my house. I covered Eddie's relationship with Peter Cross and the attempt on my life by Squeaky who was now working for Niko Cross. I chose to leave out the break-in at Daniels and the enhanced interrogation of Eddie and Peter. By now they were probably wondering about the grill marks on Eddie's ass when they complete the autopsy.

OJ sat dumbfounded for a whole minute before he

opened his mouth to start with the questions. I asked him to hold on until I shared my theory and reluctantly he agreed.

"OJ, my theory on this is that for some reason, Linebush needed money. He learned about Ortega from his son Wade and his buddies in prison. Linebush approached Ortega with a proposition. He would help Ortega import his drugs and export cash in return for offshore investments from Ortega to the Linebush companies. Eddie handled the investment side and Daniels the business side. Eddie told his lover Peter about the money and Peter told his father. Cross is also in the drug trade as confirmed by my little meeting with Peter and Georgi. Now you have two factions at odds with each other." I was trying not to rush so he could take it all in.

"Ortega figures he is not going to get his money from Linebush so he decides Roger is a loose end and shoots him. He tries to set me up to get me out of the picture. He is still trying to find Daniels for his money." Time to take a breath in order to continue my stream of consciousness.

"Also, Eddie knows a little secret about Courtney that he learned from her brother Wade. I know the secret due to being married to her for eight years. Eddie tries to blackmail Courtney and mysteriously drowns off the *Ciao Bella* where Courtney is being *held*. Courtney stands to inherit a controlling interest in Linebush LLC plus the $10 million dollar Key Man insurance policy and if Eddie is dead, the control of the estate falls to Courtney until it is settled. Motive for her and potentially for Ortega if he knows."

Now to have some fun with OJ. "I can't even begin to figure out the sexual parts of this as Courtney is married to Peter Cross, and fucking both Ortega and Niko Cross. And Eddie is fucking Peter."

OJ shakes his head as he looks at me. "Run me

through this again, Finn. This sounds like film noir at best but more like pure speculation" I took him through it again.

When I was done OJ said, "Jesus Finn, we have four dead bodies so far and in one case you are the prime suspect and in another you found the body. Now you are spinning a tale of intrigue that is convoluted to say the least. I don't even know where to begin."

"Let me help you with that part," I proposed. "As I see it, there are three issues: motive, means and opportunity. I would start with motive."

I began, "Given the mysterious death of Eddie, you can subpoena the books of his investment firm to search for irregularities. If you find questionable transactions or investments you have a potential motive for his murder and one piece of the puzzle. The same is true of Linebush. Subpoena his books to see if there is a reason for him to need money. Then you have a second piece of the puzzle. If you find problems with the Linebush books, then search his home and particularly his boat. He has a fifty-five foot Sport Fisherman the *Queen Anne's Revenge*. I suspect he's using it to smuggle drugs and money in and out of the country. Check the keel in particular."

I suggested to OJ, "Finally impound the *Ciao Bella* as a crime scene. It shouldn't raise any suspicion on Ortega's part and may keep him from leaving town."

I figured I needed OJ and the KW police to get some of these things done, as I had no way of making them happen myself. In the mean time, I was going to go after Peter Cross. What if anything was Eddie offering Peter beside the sex? How would he react if he thought Ortega had killed his lover? What had he told his father?

"OJ, I need to run but trust me, you will get all the credit if you crack this one and finally get the gold shield you deserve. I will be on my phone if you need me."

I was five minutes late for Stacy but she was already a magnet for every silver haired aging lothario at the bar in Martin's. I paused as she gently turned each down in turn for the offer of a drink and when she spotted me admiring her and her technique she smiled.

"Of all the gin joints, in all the towns, in all the world, you walk into mine," she quipped.

"I'm shocked, shocked to find that drinking is going on in this establishment," I replied.

"It is a gin joint after all," she chuckled. "But you almost lost me to that charming gentleman with the wry smile and the Amex Titanium Black Card."

I pulled out my wallet and opened it to reveal, several dusty singles and a Bank of America debit card. "Hey beautiful, can you buy a guy drink?"

"Now that's the offer I've been waiting for all evening," she replied.

I sat down beside her and ordered a Dark and Stormy for me and another Key West Sunset Martini for her. Given as it was getting toward the end of happy hour, we ordered several appetizers including the Tuna Tataki and the Lobster Medallions. While we waited, she gave me a quick update. "Well I don't have a lot but it turns out I cannot find a PADI certification for Eddie so he is not registered with them. I did not check every organization that certifies divers but PADI is the largest."

"Ok that is helpful to know. "

Our appetizers arrived and we paused to get a bit of food in us before I gave her my update.

"I spoke to OJ this afternoon and filled him in on much of what has happened so far," I mumbled between Lobster Medallions.

"Only 'much of'?" she asked.

"I left out the visits to Daniels' and Eddie's places and the *enhanced interrogation* of Eddie." I smiled at her.

"OJ is going to try to get a subpoena to search Eddie's and the Linebush offices. Also take a look at the Roger's fifty-five-foot Azimut, the *Queen Anne's Revenge*. With any luck we can get some proof that they were smuggling and laundering money."

"So where do we go from here?" she asked.

"How about dinner and a movie?" I suggested. "*Some Like it Hot* is playing at the Tropic and I thought you might like to see it."

"See it again, you mean," she said.

"So you have seen it already?" I asked.

"How do you like the shape of that liquor cabinet?" It was a quote that brought a whole new meaning to 'stocking' a liquor cabinet.

A girl who can quote from Some Like it Hot is a keeper.

"Ok, what do you have in mind?" I posed.

"How about movie then dinner at your place and we'll see what comes up."

"Stacy, this sounds like the beginning of a beautiful evening," I replied.

We headed for the Tropic for a seven p.m. start, walking along Duval. The Tropic Cinema is a local's theater that is run by volunteers. Members get discounts on movies and they sell wine by the glass or bottle to go with popcorn that is customized with various salts and cheeses like White Cheddar and Parmesan Garlic. A very civilized cinema experience. *Some Like it Hot* never disappoints and it still feels fresh even after 60 years.

~ ~ ~

My problem is that it was shot at the Hotel Del Coronado across the bridge from San Diego and I still have flashbacks of my SEAL training days. The SEAL training base is on the *Silver Strand*, a beach south of the Hotel Del. We used to do daily 4k runs along the strand from the

JSOC base to the Del. We also practiced boat-landing drills in the surf onto the rocks at the base of the hotel. Broken ankles, blown knees and even worse bodily injuries were a regular event there. The second glass of wine helped with my flashbacks.

~ ~ ~

Stacy and I grabbed a cab after the movie and headed back to my place. Crutch needed a little TLC and seemed pissed with me until he saw Stacy. Suddenly he became a sweet, loving puppy licking her hand and nuzzling her leg. She fell for it.

Being the seductive and charming host that I am, I opened a bottle of wine and we sat chatting on my sofa with Crutch curled up between us. About an hour later I took him out for his evening constitutional. He seemed to be in a hurry, which I took as a sign he liked Stacy and wanted to get back to her before she left. He was pleased when she stayed.

At seven the next morning I left Stacy sleeping and went to the White Tarpon for coffee and a breakfast sandwich to bring back for her. My regular crew was there and the talk was about the headline in the Citizen, *Prominent Local Man Dies in Prison.* I had a sinking feeling and my coffee suddenly felt like battery acid in my stomach.

I grabbed the paper and skimmed the story, then read it in more detail. Wade Linebush was found in his locked cell hanging from the bunk rail with a rope made from his sheet. The authorities at the prison were not confirming it as a suicide but speculation was that he had become depressed by the death of his father Roger and his former business partner Eddie Ransom. He had five years to go of his eight-year sentence.

The buzz at the Tarpon was that it didn't make sense. He could have been out in a year for good behavior and his sister would hire him so he could be returning to a comfortable life.

"You knew Wade well, Finn," said Dave. "Does it make any sense to you?"

I thought about it, for a second. With all that was going on in town it seemed like a hell of a coincidence. "Wade wasn't the brightest bulb in the box but his family has more money than all of us combined. A lot can happen in prison that most of us have no idea about, but the timing does seem strange to me."

First his partner Eddie, now Wade himself. Trouble is, why would anyone want him dead?" After my minimal contribution to the local gossip, I headed home to deliver breakfast to Stacy and get her take. I would never get my call to Wade.

I arrived as Stacy was stepping out of the shower. I held off on sharing the news and our breakfast got a little colder. Okay so I am a bit self-serving but it wasn't like Wade was family, at least not anymore.

Stacy was understanding and sympathetic when I shared the news. "Finn, you are a pig. How can you take advantage of me before sharing that little piece of news?"

In my defense, if you saw Stacy as she stepped out of the shower, you would understand my dilemma.

I couldn't exactly say that so I tried, "If I had mentioned it you, you might have been upset and ..."

I could see by the look on her face this approach was not working and the hole I had dug was getting deeper.

"You looked so fantastic, I completely forgot about it ... " Not working either.

"You're right, I was selfish and you looked so great ... " Better, but time to shut up. "I brought you breakfast?"

"You know were you can put that 'Sunrise Sandwich'," she suggested, "right where 'it' doesn't!" Now call me a cab and have them meet me on Duval in front of the

Gingerbread Gallery."

She grabbed the sandwich from me and stormed out of the house. At least the sandwich would not be wasted.

I called the cab and reflected on how little I understood women. Even Crutch looked at me like I was an idiot but as far as I knew he had never even been kissy-facey with another pooch over pasta.

I tried to remember the rules about how to make up after your first fight but as luck would have it my phone rang. I grabbed it and blurted, "I am really sorry. You are right. I am a pig and I just couldn't take my eyes off you coming out of the shower."

There was a pause and OJ said, "So I've been working my ass off all night following up on your story and you have been making a beast with two backs with Stacy. You're right. You *are* a pig." And he laughed.

"What the hell is a beast with two backs?" I asked not wanting to appear embarrassed by his comments.

"I forget you were an accounting major, go look it up. It's from *Othello*. It was Shakespeare's way of describing what Othello's wife Desdemona was possibly doing with a lover."

Did I mention that OJ was a smart guy? "Well *e tu brute* to you," I rejoined.

"You two lovebirds have a little tiff?" he asked. "Oh and wrong Shakespeare play by the way."

"Alright, enough. You win. Why did you call?"

"Well I was able to get a subpoena while you two were playing a Montague and a Capulet, sorry Romeo and Juliet. I searched Eddie's office after the break-in but didn't expect to find much. We are searching Linebush's office and boat as we speak. Seems a judge was more receptive this morning after Wade showed up dead."

"When do you think you will have anything from the searches?" I asked.

"Come on Finn, you know these take time. I'll let you know at the end of the day if anything obvious shows up," he promised. I bid him adieu.

Crutch at this point was dancing around on his back legs and begging for a fluid adjustment break. It seemed like a good time to take him around the block and go for a ride to clear my head.

After his usual dozen or so *stop and sniffs* he took care of business and pranced back to the house. We hopped on my bike and rode the wrong way up Catherine Street for a block as we headed for the White Street pier.

The ocean has a calming effect on me and I am reminded that nature is indifferent to human foibles and drama. Long after I am gone, waves will still lap on whatever beach remains after global climate change floods the Keys. We live in an earthly paradise I think could be the Garden of Eden and while hardly a biblical scholar, I can see that as man's knowledge increases, he seems to be destroying paradise. Knowledge doesn't necessarily mean understanding.

Ok enough of the new age, where have all the flowers gone reflections. I only have a limited time on this Rock and right now we have lost two of the three last members of one of the most prominent families in the town with my ex-wife the last remaining.

The last remaining ...

CHAPTER TWENTY-TWO

HOLY SHIT, could she be the next victim or maybe, actually the killer.

I just couldn't see Courtney as a killer but I know she can be very manipulative. She is sleeping with Cross and he thinks he is going to have a kid with her. I suspect that Ortega is a killer given the death of Alexi and I suspect Cross is capable of it given the death of the unknown body found off Smathers.

Could Courtney have plotted with Ortega to kill Linebush and have Wade killed in jail? She ends up with the estate free and clear and there is no proof. Why would Ortega ...? Money ...?

Ortega was looking for Daniels after he disappeared, trying to collect money. How much money is involved? And is it enough to kill three people? As I started to ride back to drop off Crutch and grab a Bloody Mary from Cindy, I suddenly stopped. If I went to Courtney and shared the idea that Ortega was responsible for the deaths of Roger and Wade, how would she respond? It seemed like a reasonable plan to flush out some additional information.

~ ~ ~

I decided to skip the Bloody Mary and went home to call Courtney. I tried her old cell number and surprisingly she picked up. "Courtney, it's Finn. I just heard about Wade and I wanted to let you know I am so sorry," I said disingenuously.

"Finn, you didn't give a shit about Wade or you wouldn't have put him in jail. I blame you as much as anyone for his death and you can go fuck yourself." She hung up. What is it about this family and hanging up?

I waited a few minutes and called her back. "Courtney, before you hang up, hear me out. I am concerned for your safety."

"What the fuck are you talking about?" she asked.

"I am concerned that both your father and Wade are now dead and you are the last person left in the family. Is there anyone who stands to benefit from your death?"

She paused and seemed to be thinking about it. "Why would you think that Finn?" she asked.

Ok it was now time to offer up the bait.

"Courtney, your Dad called me when you were being held hostage by Ortega. Ortega wanted me to find Daniels and it doesn't take a rocket scientist to figure out it was about money. Clearly Daniels knew something and Ortega wanted him found. Your father is dead and it wasn't me that killed him and now Wade is dead. It seems a fair assumption that Ortega is going to come after you to get what ever he thinks he is owed."

Again there was a pause as she seemed to consider my logic. "Finn, are you saying that you think Ortega was responsible for my Dad's death?" she asked.

"Yes and perhaps he was involved with Wade's as well," I suggested.

"The prison said his death looked like a suicide," Courtney offered.

"I know but I think there might be more to it. I'm sure Ortega has contacts in the prison and could have made some calls. I just think you need to be careful. Do you think you can convince him that I am still looking for Daniels to buy me some time?"

Then I had to add, "And by the way, why haven't you reported the kidnapping to the KW police and the possibility of Ortega shooting your Dad? And why have you been freed?"

"Leave it alone, Finn." She said. "You were not able to find Daniels in time so I made a deal with Ortega to settle his investment with us and I don't want him to come after me, so just drop it."

I paused. "Are you telling me that you know he killed your father and you are going to let it go?"

I heard her voice choke up as she said, "Of course not but until I can prove something there is no point in going after him. I need to bury my Dad, and now Wade, then try to figure out what to do. Now please just drop it." And she hung up again.

Now that was an interesting call. She knows or at least suspects Ortega is responsible for her Dad's death and maybe Wade's. She is saying she is being threatened by Ortega and has agreed to settle a debt of some kind. Now if she is working with Ortega, she will let him know that I now know at least something is off and he will probably come after me. If she *isn't* working with him, then how will she handle it?

I have just become *the tethered goat* but who is going to come after me?

As I pondered this dilemma, my phone rang and when I answered, it was Stacy. "So to what do I owe the pleasure of this call from my lover, I mean my lawyer?" I queried.

"Finn, you are incorrigible, and besides I am not talking to you."

"Oh right, so how can I help you, Ms. ...? "

"I thought I would do a little digging and made some calls on your behalf to an assistant DA buddy of mine in Miami. I thought you might like to know that they are about to declare Wade's death a homicide. It seems his neck was broken before he was found appearing to hang himself in his cell."

On the one hand, I was glad she was now at least speaking to me and on the other it confirmed my suspicion that Wade had been killed. Now the question was *who done it* or *who had it done?*

"Stacy, listen thanks. I also want to apologize for my behavior this morning. It was thoughtless and selfish." I shut up and waited. She said, "You're right it was, but you are so adorable that I can't stay angry with you."

Not really. She actually said, "No Finn you are still a pig and I am not ready to forgive you." And she hung up. *I seem to be having that effect on women these days.*

~ ~ ~

I decided to really stir things up in advance of the funeral for Roger and now Wade Linebush set for tomorrow at St Paul's by calling Peter Cross.

It took a couple of tries but after about ten minutes he answered. "Peter, it's Finn Pilar. I just wanted to extend my condolences on Eddie's death. I know you were," I paused, "*close.*"

"What the fuck are you talking about Pilar?" he exclaimed.

"I'm sorry, I thought you knew."

"Knew what?"

"The police took a body off a boat yesterday and it has been tentatively identified as Eddie."

"You are so full of shit Pilar. Eddie hates the water, he wouldn't go even close to a boat."

I was gobsmacked.

If not Eddie, who? And where was Eddie?

"Peter, I don't know what to say. You may want to track down Eddie or go out to the county morgue and try to see if you recognize the body." I hung up then called OJ.

"OJ, I just had an odd call with Peter Cross who was a *friend* of Eddie Ransom. He said Eddie wouldn't get caught dead on a boat as he was afraid of the water. "Are there any identifying marks on the body that can be confirmed as belonging to him?"

"Like what, Finn?" OJ asked.

"I don't know. Moles, birth marks, scars, tattoos, you know the usual."

"No, but we have sent his fingerprints into IAFIS for identification and we should know more in the next day or so."

IAFIS is the Integrated Automated Fingerprint Identification System that is used to check fingerprints. If Eddie had ever been printed, then a record should be there.

"Have you been able to find any family that might be able to identify him?" I inquired.

"So far no. Listen, why are you asking? Is this part of that discussion we had yesterday?"

"Yea, it seems strange that the body is hard to identify. It was found by the crew of *Ciao Bella* and he is or was in line to run the Linebush estate. Things are just not adding up and if it's not Eddie, who is it?"

I was about to hang up when OJ said, "By the way I was going to call you but got busy. We finished our search of Eddie's office and we have found something interesting."

Now he had my attention. "Yes?"

"It seems that Eddie was managing a rather large account for Linebush."

"How large?" I asked.

"Really large, like $25 million large"

"Holy shit, really?"

"Yea, it seems that an outside investor sent regular investment payments from the Caymans into the Linebush corporate account. It looks like draw downs on a committed investment into his company and to date it is $25 mil."

"Are there any documents to show who is investing or the terms of the investment?" I asked.

"No, not that we have found so far but we are still looking at the Linebush corporate offices," OJ offered.

"There has to be a record of the share distributions in the company's books and some track on when this started."

"We are looking into all this but so far no joy, and with Linebush and Eddie both dead it is going to be tough to dig through this stuff. $25 million is a lot of money."

"Yea, and a lot of motive," I posed.

"Finn, before you jump to any conclusions, let's see what the evidence shows. Remember, if we draw conclusions too soon we can start to make the evidence fit the conclusion, not the other way around."

"Fuck off, OJ. I was the one that taught you that one. Tell me what other *conclusions* you are considering."

"Oh, just chill Finn, you don't need to go all rabid dog on me. I am just reminding you that this is a high profile case involving the Key West gentry and we need to be deliberate and follow the process."

I had had enough of the step-by-step, piece-by-piece casework and wanted to shake the bushes a bit.

"Look OJ, you need to look more closely at Eddie's death. I can't say why, but something is not right. Linebush dies; murdered. Wade dies under questionable circumstances. Eddie is the trustee of the Linebush estate and in charge of his estate and business. Now he dies by accident. Who benefits?" I wondered out loud.

"My bet is Courtney," I proposed.

"Finn, I can't believe you're suggesting that Courtney is involved in this in some way. We are talking about her father and her brother for God's sakes."

I thought about this some more. It seemed like she had a very clear motive - taking over the family company. Having said that, if Ortega is the mystery investor in the company, he has $25 mil *or more* reasons to make sure she is in a position to pay him back, with or without her knowing he is involved.

Courtney could be a coldhearted bitch; okay, I am the embittered ex who she threw over when I arrested her brother, but I could not see her as a killer. She has a good life and no real reason to kill her family other than maybe for more money. But it just doesn't fit.

I told OJ I needed some time to give this more thought and asked him to call me if he learned anything more about Eddie's death.

I grabbed Crutch's leash and decided to walk down to Martin's for Happy Hour. I called Stacy but got voicemail so left a message to see if she could join me for dinner.

~ ~ ~

Duval Street *in season* can be a mad house, even at the upper end and today was no exception. Cruise ships disgorge about 2,000 tourists each onto Key West streets and there can be as many as three ships docked on some days. I love my adopted city but some days I can't decide if I am just a visitor to Disney World South or one of the exhibits.

I suppose a three-legged dog is an attraction but he can slow you down on a walk as people stop to pet him. He breaks into his routine usually at the corner of Duval and Truman for the few tourists that actually wait for the light to change. It usually includes a high five for a kid standing at the light, then a low five, rolling over and now his back flip although he still can't stick the landing. It could even save the kid's life as parents seem to think the lights are for locals only. It is usually good for a few bucks that I use to buy Crutch a beer. I guess we look like we need it.

~ ~ ~

We got to Martins for happy hour and I ordered a Lemontini and a Black Forest Salad. Crutch got his usual light beer and lamb chops. We both need to watch our waistlines. While I waited for Stacy to call back, I sipped my perfectly poured martini and thought some more about Courtney.

If not Courtney, then who? The only options I could think of were Ortega, Eddie, and .... suddenly, I thought of Daniels.

Daniels knew the company finances and had access to the company accounts at Eddie's firm; he had been missing for almost 10 days; and who was he anyway? What if he actually had skipped town with his family and the money? Twenty five million can be a big motivator.

I called Matt.

"Hey Dude, how goes it?" he answered.

"You know me," I said. "Still making the island safe for snow birds. Actually, I am doing my best to scare them off to cut down on the crowds. What we really need is another oil spill."

He laughed out loud. "I don't imagine this is a social call so what's up?" he asked.

"You are really getting this detective thing nailed down. Actually, I could use some help. I need to see if you can track down Shawn Daniels, the Linebush CFO. The last I had on him was a neighbor who said he had gone to Orlando with his kids. And that was about eight days ago. Five days at Mickey World seems a bit much even for a CFO in need of a distraction for his rug rats. I am wondering if you can dig up something on his background and try to track him down."

Matt paused and said, "Is that all you have on him; name, rank and rug rats? Details to follow?"

"I will fax my notes on my search so far and see if you can track him down. I have a hinky feeling about this guy."

"Ok, I will look into it and see what I can find," he promised. "I'll be in touch."

As I hung up, I ordered my second Lemontini and was

lost in thought when Stacy came in and sat on the stool next to me.

"Fuck off and order me a drink," she said without even looking at me.

"And you're looking lovely this evening too," I fawned while waving at Luca the bartender. "Luca can you bring my lawyer a *White Flag* please; two shots of lemon Grey Goose, a shot of mea culpa and a dash of forgiveness. Ice cold, straight up and hold the twist."

I glanced over at her and asked, "Did I get that right?"

"You left out the *I'm an asshole* around the rim."

I broke up and she smiled.

"Right. Did you get that Luca?" Being the smart bartender that he is, he made it a double.

I waited for her to take a sip.

"So what are we doing here, Finn?"

"You mean besides enjoying ... "

"Don't say it."

"I was only going to say, "besides enjoying a martini." I lied

"You are full of shit, Finn. What's up?"

Don't you just love this girl?

"If you mean besides just wanting to see you, then yes I thought you might be able to help with a little problem."

She waved at Luca for another round. It appeared the *White Flag* was having an impact.

"And what little problem might that be?" she asked.

I suggested it was best discussed in a quieter setting and reluctantly she agreed to move over to the dining room inside.

We ordered the 'Grouper Dijon' and a nice bottle of La Spinetta Rose. While we waited I laid out my theory.

"This case has been getting more and more complicated by the day," I began. "The disappearance of Daniels, the *kidnapping* of Courtney and Roger, rumors of drugs, lost and found treasure, two bodies showing up randomly and now a third body suspected of being Eddie plus Roger and Wade dead. It now looks like $25 million is in play with Ortega still searching for it."

"Ok I get the picture," she said.

"Now here is my theory. I suspect that the body that was found and thought to be Eddie will turn out to not have burn marks on its ass. If that is the case, then who is it? I am going to bet it is Daniels."

Stacy had a look of shock on her face. "You're kidding right?"

"Let me finish. What if Eddie and Daniels both knew the money was coming into Linebush as an *investment* helping bail out Roger. Roger needed cash after Wade went to prison and his Ponzi scheme collapsed so he lets Courtney in on the little family treasure secret. She decides to help herself to the treasure and Ortega who is the investor, looses out and gets pissed. He comes after Roger so Roger points the finger at Daniels to buy time, hence I come in to search for Daniels."

Stacy cocks her head to the side to listen better I guess.

"Roger thinking he has $25 million with Eddie goes to Eddie to get his money. Eddie and Daniels have helped themselves to a little windfall while claiming the money is gone after some bad investments. Roger is screwed; no money, no treasure. Ortega, trying to get his money back kills Roger then Wade, to scare Courtney. She agrees to pay him back using the treasure."

Stacy flips her hair back so seductively I almost lose my train of thought but I surprisingly collect myself.

"Eddie, needing a fall guy, calls Daniels and tells him the coast is clear and Daniels comes back to Key West. I suspect the body in the morgue is not Eddie, but Daniels. Eddie will show up claiming he was away on a mini vacation at Little Palm Island all shocked and surprised about events and with $25 mil socked away in a Cayman account."

"Jesus Finn. You should write a book. That is the weirdest thing I have ever heard and you left out the two random bodies, the drugs and the Cross family. How does all that tie in?"

"Ok so it's not perfect but it does tie together a lot of stuff," I said defensively.

"Oh don't get all whiney on me. I am not saying you are wrong but how are you going to prove it?"

"Well I'm working on it. And that is where you come in." I laid out my plan and she laughed.

Our dinner arrived and we had a great meal together. She was coming around. Being the gentleman that I am and not wanting to push my luck, I kissed her on the cheek and told her I would pick her up in three hours.

With Matt looking for Daniels, I figured I needed to find Eddie. I figured my first stop was Peter Cross. He had sounded truly shocked that Eddie was dead and in the morgue but did he actually go to the morgue to check it out? Also, I needed to see if the body in the morgue was actually Eddie and I was probably the only one other than Peter who could identify him knowing about the origins of those burn marks on his ass. It would be closed now but I had a long night ahead if I was going to get this resolved. As a first step I needed to prove that a treasure existed.

CHAPTER TWENTY-THREE

THE *QUEEN ANNE'S REVENGE* was docked at a slip in the harbor off A&B Lobster House restaurant near the Galleon Resort and Marina. I knew that OJ was checking the keel to see if it could have been used to smuggle items in and out of the country, but I wanted to look at the GPS. I picked up Stacy at midnight and we drove down to the Hyatt on Front Street and parked.

Dressed in black, we strolled along the docks looking like a pair of slightly drunk lovers stopping to look at all the boats. I had a thumb drive in my pocket. Once we spotted the *Queen Anne*, we walked passed it glancing over to see if anyone was on board as well as on the neighboring boats. All appeared quiet as we passed it a second time and I looked for alarms that might go off if I went on board.

I figured the boat had been taken apart by OJ and his team but they might not have known what to look for. As a member of the family, so to speak, I knew that Roger was obsessive about his GPS Logger. He kept it to track and record his favorite fishing spots and I suspected one of them was the treasure spot. If I could compare where he went with known treasure sites I might find one that was similar on his recordings. With Stacy keeping a lookout several boats down, I crept aboard the *Queen Anne's Revenge*.

Key West is a relatively safe harbor with minimal security. The rope barrier that separates the private dock from the public ones has only a brass hook to hold its *Owners and Guests Only* sign in place.

Most owners just lock the sliders to the salons but I knew that Roger use to keep a spare key in a small magnetic case in the sunscreen basket on the outdoor bar. A quick look showed that nothing had changed in the three years since Courtney and I had split.

I slipped into the salon and went straight to the navigation station and chart table. With the advent of GPS, few people use charts anymore but Roger was old school and kept a bunch on board.

The Logger was right where it was always kept inside the table. I powered it up and plugged my thumb drive into the USB port and began downloading the history of the boat's travels. After about three minutes the data dump was done and I packed up. Easy peazy.

As I turned to leave, a shadow flickered in the corner of my eye and I felt the cold steel of a knife at my throat. For a moment, nothing was said.

"Hand it over Finn," Courtney finally said. "One more body is not going to matter given the count that's been racked up over the last eight days."

Nothing is more frightening than a razor sharp blade held a hair from your carotid. Just a slight twitch and you can bleed out in a little as two minutes.

"Chill babe, I am just looking for the old GPS that I left here when we split. I finally remembered where I left it is and ... "

"Finn you are so full of shit. Hand it over with the thumb drive as well."

"No problem," I sighed. There are days when courage just doesn't kick start with the rest of your brain cells, and then it arrives with a vengeance. With my left hand I reached into my pocket to get the thumb drive and leaned forward slightly. As the knife moved forward with my lean and my left hand came out of my pocket and up to pass her the drive, my right hand shot up and grabbed her wrist and my head snapped back and grazed her nose just enough to stop her in her tracks.

She cried out and tried to slash my throat but my right hand had her wrist and the knife moved uselessly away from its intended target.

The pain of even a slight hit to the nose is sharp and intense. It took the fight out of her and with a firm twist of her tiny wrist, she was forced to drop the knife. It may seem a bit of overkill but a knife to the throat does get the juices flowing.

She knelt on the deck of the boat with a sob. "Finn, I need that thumb drive or I am going to be dead," she whimpered.

Now I am a softy at heart so I simply said, "You have a hell of a way of asking for my help."

"What? You would have just handed it over to me if I asked politely?" she sniffed. "Right."

Ok, so she had a point.

"So sit down and explain what the fuck is going on."

She sniffled and sobbed but basically told me at least part of the truth. "After Wade went to jail, thanks to you asshole, Dad grew more and more worried. He kept talking about needing money. It had never been a problem before that point. It seemed that Dad had been feeding Wade money to bail him out of the Ponzi scheme with the investors at the marina. Dad's business was also in need of cash to finish up the hotels and the road project and it was all coming to a head at the same time.

So far so good on her part.

"Eddie was supposed to manage the company accounts in a conservative way but it turned out he was a shitty investment advisor and had lost big in the markets. Dad's accounts were down millions after the '08 crash and Eddie had chased the markets down losing more and more on margin. Dad grew desperate but he knew as a last resort he could access our secret stash of emeralds and ..."

"Whoooooa, slow down. What secret stash of

emeralds?"

"Oh right, I didn't know about this when we were together. Anyway, he knew if we needed it, we could fall back on it and ... "

"Courtney, you are ducking the secret stash thing. Go back."

"Alright. Are you familiar with the *Nuestra Senora de Atocha*?"

"Sure, you can't live in Key West without knowing the story."

"Well you are probably not familiar with the *Nuestra Senora del Rosario*."

"You're right, what the hell is that?"

"Well in September of 1622, you know the *Atocha* was wrecked on a reef about twenty miles west of Key West. What you may not know, is that it was part of a fleet that consisted of twenty-eight ships. Five were lost but only three have been located."

"Ok, I'm with you so far."

"Well my great-grandfather Enoch, located treasure almost a hundred years ago. It turned out to be from one of the ships previously thought found, the *Nuestra Senora del Rosario*. It was originally thought to be salvaged but it turns out that the crew had dumped gold and silver chests to lighten the ship during the storm and get it off the reef. Enoch found the dumped chests long before Mel Fisher found the *Atocha*."

"Why am I just learning about this now?"

"Finn, you are now one of only two people alive who knows about this discovery. Old Grandpa Enoch was a shrewd and larcenous wrecker who knew if he told anyone about the find, he would be hounded for the rest of his life and never be able to harvest it in the way he wanted to."

"How the hell have you kept this a secret for so long?" I asked.

"Part of the problem was that the treasure was in about fifty feet of water and only about ten miles off the coast. He stumbled on it when he was blown onto a reef in a storm and his boat sank. He was trying to salvage what he could of his own boat after the storm and lo and behold he found some coins embedded in a silver bar. His boat was at the limits of free diving so he marked it with a lobster pot float and went home to figure out his next steps.

About a week later, or so the story goes, he went back and moved his marker two hundred yards due east of the sunset on that day and dropped an anchor on the spot. He then tied a sturdy line to a pot buoy and went back to the spot where the treasure was found. He knew he could find the exact spot every year on that date by the position of the buoy and the spot where the sun went down."

Courtney reached over to physically close my opened mouth.

"For the next twenty years, he would go out to the spot every year and harvest his treasure and then ignore it for the rest of the year. On his death bed, he told my grandfather who then told my father who then passed it on to my brother when Dad could no longer dive for it."

I was trying to think of something smart-ass to say but nothing would come to mind so I just let Courtney continue.

"Dad was even cagier than old Enoch and when he found a bag with about seventy-five pounds of emeralds, he decided to stop going to the site every year and just slowly filter the emeralds into the market as treasure emeralds without revealing the ship they came from. He didn't get the *Atocha* premium but he still had a stash worth millions."

"Enough details Courtney. What's the bottom line?"

"Ok, the bottom line is the emeralds were sold off to

cover losses in the business and I hope to find the treasure site with the GPS to pay off Ortega and company debt due. With Dad dead, it is the only way to make up the loss and save the Linebush companies."

I took a minute to absorb all this to decide what to ask. "Courtney, you said after you asked me so nicely, if you don't get this GPS you are dead, right? So banks are not generally in the business of killing a business owner who is behind on a loan. I know this as I am still around and I owe money to half the banks in town. To whom do you owe money?"

"I can't say or he'll kill you too," she murmured.

"So you are not going to tell me to save my life, yet fifteen minutes ago you were going to kill me to get the GPS."

"Finn, I'm desperate. I have to find the stash. I think he is the one responsible for Dad's death and possibly for Wade's."

"Look Courtney, you have filled in some of the gaps in a scheme that I had begun to suspect was going on but I can't help you if you don't tell me the name of the guy pulling the strings."

"Finn, I mean it. If I tell you, he will kill you too."

"She's right Mr. Pilar," a deep menacing voice behind me said. "But now I'll be forced to kill you anyway as I'm sure you know."

The hair on the back of my neck stood up and I almost had a warm stream running down my leg. Shit, I thought, this is not good.

"Don't turn around," the voice continued, "and put your hands behind your back."

Slowly I put my hands behind my back and felt the flex cuffs slip onto my wrists.

"Now kneel down next to Courtney," he said.

I was feeling sick as I looked up and saw how wrong I had been. I felt the needle stick in my neck and my vision immediately began to blur. "Yo ..." I mumbled as my head dropped to the floor.

CHAPTER TWENTY-FOUR

WHEN I CAME TO, I could feel the motion of the boat. I had a grade A+ hangover although I could not remember drinking a lot and my hands were cuffed behind my back. I could not for the life of me remember any of it. The sun was coming up so I knew I had been out for at least six hours and if you count time to get the boat ready for departure and for clearing the harbor without attracting attention, we had been at sea for as much as five hours. With this boat we could be fifty miles out in about twenty directions.

The boat was bouncing along at speed and I was bouncing with it. As I looked around I could see a hooded figure at the helm but when I tried to stand, I found myself tied to a stainless rail stanchion on the port side.

As I lay in the well of the back deck trying to recall what had happened and how I had gotten here, it came back in a jumble of snap shots. I realized I had been an idiot, no surprise. How had I missed the signs? All the time I had been focused on Ortega when in fact it was Niko Cross, the guy on the edges -- the one just out of sight. Suddenly it all made sense. Now I just needed to get back to land and prove it all.

As the boat began to slow, I realized this would not be good. While I continued to act unconscious, my mind raced to figure out the next step. Would they just tie an anchor to my feet and toss me over or would they want it to look like an accident and untie me first, then toss me over?

As I lay there watching through almost closed eyes, the guy with the hoodie slowed the boat to a crawl and came back to the well where I lay. He reached into one of the lockers covered by a seat cushion and hauled out a fifty-five pound Bruce anchor with a length of chain attached. He pulled a padlock from his hoodie pocket. It was clear I was going to be chasing an anchor to the bottom, however deep that might be.

Rather than attach the chain to my legs first, he began by untying me from the rail stanchion leaving my hands cuffed behind my back. As he reached back to get the chain to tie to my legs, I kicked out against the side of the well and slid across the deck. He was surprised but not for long. He jumped up at the same time I scrambled to my feet. He reached behind and pulled a knife from the small of his back and began advancing warily toward me. I started to hyperventilate which he took as nerves and he chuckled.

Now a fifty-mile swim with my hands cuffed behind my back was not the greatest idea, but it seemed better than a knife in the chest. My plan was to let him charge me with the knife and turn at the last second to slip the knife and then lunge with the two of us going over together. We plan; again God laughs.

He almost missed with the knife but turned at the last second and caught the edge of my hip with the blade. The part of the plan that worked, was that I was able to hook my knee on his leg and we both went over together, me taking a final very deep breath before diving down to about ten feet.

Now most people are not aware of it, but part of Navy SEAL and EOD training includes Pool Comprehensive or 'Pool Comp' during the dive phase of BUD/S. One of the more fun exercises, in my view, was the underwater swim with your hands and feet tied. I knew that I could hold my breath for at least two minutes and swim about fifty meters so I could probably outlast him underwater. Before

I took off on my pleasure swim, I needed to see if he had dropped the knife.

As I spun around in a circle under the boat I spotted him doing the same. It looked like I finally got lucky as he did not have the knife. I smiled as he rose to the surface for air. I swam as fast as I could with my arms tied behind my back until I reached the bow of the boat. I went up for air and re-submerged.

In BUD/S, not only did we have to swim fifty meters with hands and feet tied, but we also needed to get our hands back in front of us by slipping them under our butts and then forcing our feet through. It is not easy but it's doable and it was the second time in a week that I had to do it. If I survived this little episode I needed to thank my BUD/S instructor personally.

Now with my hands in front I dove back down just in time to see him do the same but this time he had a long stick in his hands. *What the fuck is that about?* Then I saw the mini yellow Spare Air canister in his mouth. *Oh shit.*

It wasn't a stick but a spear gun. *I could be screwed.* He dove toward me and I dove deeper.

The Navy trains the SEALs to be the best underwater combat swimmers in the world and even though I had to DOR from BUD/S after Second Phase, it was not pool comp that almost killed me. In fact I loved that part.

It is amazing what warp speed thoughts go through your head when you see a guy with a spear gun coming at you. I was transported back to Fleming Key where I trained at the Combat Dive School and first fell in love with Key West. One of the requirements is to free dive thirty meters or ninety feet in the dive tank. Then I warp-speeded back to the situation at hand. What is the range of the gun and how good a swimmer is this guy?

I remembered that a spear gun is only really accurate to about two to three meters but that is when it is trying to shoot a small fish. If I could get and stay out of range and go deep, I might be able to avoid becoming a speared grouper and if I was really lucky, get him to go too deep while trying to catch me.

I dove and he followed. *Now it was a test, skill or be killed.*

Could he get close enough to spear me, not run out of air and then re-surface without bursting a lung? Could I get deep enough to both tempt him to keep coming and yet stay out of range?

We dove.

Now ninety feet does not seem like a lot but the water pressure at that depth is about forty pounds per square inch on the human body. Compare that with ten feet where it is about four pounds per square inch. I would not recommend trying this at home folks. You really need to equalize your ears or blow a drum and if you come up too fast after breathing compressed air without equalizing, you can burst a lung.

We dove.

As I began to reach my limit, I glanced back and at that moment he fired the spear gun. The shaft came lancing at me and I could see the tip and the barb heading my way. The shock cord stopped it inches from my nose and I grabbed the spear. I yanked hard pulling it out of his hands. He had fired too soon and was now racing for the surface. I emphasize racing because I knew at that moment I had him. I slowly began my ascent while reloading the spear gun. As I rose I could see him fighting to surface for air. I continued my measured ascent.

I spotted the boat to my left and made a slight course correction to surface on the opposite side to my dive buddy/ killer. As I broke the surface, I could hear him yelling to his partner on board that he needed help. While I was cuffed, I could still use my arms. I fired the reloaded spear gun and hit him in the chest. His partner Courtney, *my once loving wife*, came down to the swim platform and without asking what happened to her ex-husband, began to help the hunter up onto the teak. Okay, so we weren't exactly on the best of terms but a flicker of concern would have been nice.

Courtney pulled off the ski mask that had been obscuring the diver's face and I realized that my would-be murderer was Peter Cross. No wonder he was willing to extend himself to dive as deep as he did to get me. He hated my guts after that little stove episode on his lover Eddie's ass. Of course, his old man Niko was not a big fan of mine either.

I hovered underneath the bottom of the swim platform that was about three inches above the surface and watched as Courtney helped him out of the water. He was bleeding from his nose and ears and coughing up blood from his chest wound. *He was fucked.*

To my surprise, she at first tried to help him but it was not going well. He lay on the platform bleeding out. She stood there not seeming to know what to do. Suddenly she leaned over and pushed him back in the water. *Holy shit.*

Peter struggled and tried to speak as he began to drift away from the boat and she stood there watching him. He was looking at her and in the last second before he sank beneath the surface, he saw me clinging to the underside of the swim platform.

Serves you right you fucker. Did I mention I can be a cold-hearted prick at times?

Courtney looked around to see if there were any other boats in the area then headed for the cockpit. As she started the engines I climbed awkwardly to the platform and prepared for a long, wet, bumpy ride.

As we started moving, I reached up to the life ring on the back stanchion and pulled it off with its attached

EPIRB. I guess I'm not totally heartless after all. Maybe Peter could get it and hang on. The EPIRB would help locate him.

In the meantime, I could use this pleasant outing to try and sort out loose ends of what was now looking like a solvable puzzle.

The knife wound on my hip was bleeding but not seriously so I began to develop a plan. If I slipped off the boat as we entered Key West Harbor, Courtney would not know that I was still alive. She would probably tell Niko that I had killed Peter and she had left me out in the ocean wounded and probably dead. It left her free to go after the remaining treasure, pay off Ortega and presto change-o, she is now in charge of the Linebush companies with Ortega out of the picture. She and Cross could ride off in the sunset.

Wait a minute. Why bother to pay Ortega? Why not somehow blame him for the death of Peter and get Niko to kill him? She then has all the treasure for her own use, potentially a nice little money laundering business *and* drug dealer Niko as a lover. *Even better.*

As we began heading to the slips near A&B Lobster and as the sun was going down, I dropped off the stern of the boat and swam awkwardly to the docks near the Conch Republic Seafood Company. I found a beer bottle on the street, this never being a problem in Key West, and broke it into a garbage bin. *I may be a killer, but I don't litter.* I cut off the flex cuffs with the broken bottleneck then called Stacy.

"Finn, what the fuck happened? Are you okay? Where have you been?" It was nice to hear that she was concerned.

"It's a long story, Stac. I need to disappear for a bit. Can you come by with your car and take me back to your place?" I asked.

"Finn, is this your idea of trying to get back in bed with me? If it is, you are SOL asshole."

"Wait, wait, Stac, let me explain when I see you. The idea of getting back in your bed never occurred to me." I paused, "Well, it might have occurred to me, but it is not the motive for staying at your place." I paused again. "Well not the primary motive." I was digging a deeper hole by the minute.

"Shut up Finn, where are you? I'll be there as quick as I can."

"Thanks, I'm in the alley between the Boathouse and the Conch Republic. If you come into the Conch Republic parking area, I will meet you there."

"Got it. I'll be there in ten minutes."

We hung up and my next call was to Matt.

"Where the fuck have you been? Dude. Your girl friend has been calling me every fifteen minutes to see if I had heard from you."

"Long story and at the moment I am presumed dead."

"Well you sound like shit but if you're dead then you sound pretty good."

I smiled and explained what I needed. Just before I hung up he said, "Call me back when you get settled. We need to talk about Daniels."

The dark clothes that I had worn the previous night had dried in the heat that still emanated from the pavement after another ninety-degree day on The Rock.

When Stacy arrived, I did my best slink out to her car and jumped into the back seat, lay down on the floor and said with my best Sean Connery accent, "Drive around the island Mish Money Penny, and make shure we're not followed."

She laughed then purred, "Whatever you say, Mr. Bond."

As she drove, I outlined what happened during the last

eighteen hours after I went aboard the *Queen Anne's Revenge.* She filled me on her day after seeing Niko and Peter go aboard the boat as I was searching it and then the boat pulling out of the harbor with me apparently on it. She had tried to track it but they had disconnected the radio and the vessel-tracking unit. She had then called Matt hoping he could help but was unable to reach him. Finally, she figured I was a big boy and could handle my self. Niko had not played a role in any of my conspiracy scenarios so I was probably okay. She decided to take care of Crutch and wait for me to call.

We got back to her place after about thirty minutes of driving around the island through Old Town lanes and alleys finally arriving at Stock Island. She even checked around her house by the golf course to make sure she was not being watched and finally we settled in her kitchen with a large dry martini for me and a white wine for her.

I called Matt. "So what's the scoop with Daniels?" I asked.

"Well it took some real digging but it seems our Mr. Daniels has been a very busy boy."

"How so?" I asked.

"Well, let me take you back a bit first. It seems that Mr. Daniels, the doting father of two and husband of loving wife ... is not really Shawn Daniels."

CHAPTER TWENTY-FIVE

"YOU'RE SHITTING ME!" I blurted.

"Yea I am making this up to screw with your head" he replied sarcastically. "Actually I couldn't make this up," he chuckled "It seems according to my sources that he is Daniel Beaner, a material witness and former accountant for a drug cartel in Brownsville, Texas. He testified against the family in a case seven years ago and then disappeared. Everyone thought he had been taken out by the family but in fact, he was in the witness protection program."

"How the hell did you figure that out?" I asked.

"You mean besides being a detective?" he retorted.

"Smart ass. Start talking."

"You may recall that during the first Gulf War, I was with SEAL Team 3 and we were deployed as *forward observers* near Bagdad. One night we got a call from some Marines who were in a jam and we went in and *observed* for them. I have stayed in touch with a couple of guys on the team and it turns out one is now a U.S. Marshal. He has helped me a couple of times in the past and I asked if he knew of anyone named Daniels. He got back to me yesterday and filled me in."

"And?"

"It turns out our Mr. Daniels has to check in every two weeks with a Marshal just to keep tabs on him and make sure he is still okay. Mr. Daniels missed his last check-in and it seems he has disappeared. Then last week his prints showed up in a search for an I.D. on a body found in the waters off Key West. Ring a bell?"

"Son of a bitch!" I exclaimed. "So the body isn't Eddie, it's Daniels!"

"The Marshals are looking into it but they suspect that the cartel finally found out where *Daniels* ended up and hired Ortega to make him disappear. My bet is Ortega had Daniels all along and was just squeezing old man Linebush and Courtney for repayment of the investment he had made in Linebush's company. Daniels probably told him the cash in the accounts had been lost and Ortega needed to get money somewhere else from Linebush."

"So the obvious question is where the hell is Eddie?" I asked.

"Now that is a good question. Until you told me about your adventures with Peter Cross, I figured they were in a cabin somewhere sitting on a shitload of cash from the company accounts and playing hid the sausage again. Now with Peter dead, I am not sure what the hell is happening," Matt puzzled.

"If I was a betting man, I would say, Eddie is hanging out on Ortega's boat waiting for things to sort out with the I.D. of Daniels. Then he will reappear claiming that he did not know everyone thought he was missing. Ortega has his money back from Eddie who emptied the accounts and Eddie is still in charge of the Linebush companies until the old man's estate is settled."

"Ok, so how does all this fit together with Niko Cross and Courtney?" Matt questioned.

"This is still all about the old blood feud between these two families," I suggested. Linebush needed money, as his treasure horde was dry thanks to Wade's Ponzi scheme. Ortega steps in as an investor and suddenly Linebush is in the drug trade. Niko sees his drug interests threatened by his old rival and sends a message to Ortega by killing one of his men. Now the game is on."

"So now what?" Matt asked.

"I have a plan but I may need you here to back me up. It's going to get dicey." *What a shock that must have come to Matt.*

"Ok, so what's your plan?"

I went over it and he chuckled, "You are one ballsy dude, dude. I'll be able to make it down by tomorrow."

With that he hung up and I told Stacy it was time for bed ... to sleep. I was injured, after all ...

"I made up the couch," she smiled.

When my face dropped, she smiled seductively. "Just kidding."

I slept well that night.

~ ~ ~

I wanted to give Courtney and Niko time to talk. Does he think I am dead? Does he know Peter is probably dead?

In the morning, Matt showed up and we put the plan into action. Matt placed a call to Niko Cross. He told him that Stacy and I had been over at the *Queen Anne's Revenge* two nights ago and gone aboard to pick up my lost GPS unit. Stacy had waited at Alonzo's Oyster Bar and saw he and Peter board the boat. She saw Niko get off a few minutes later but there was no sign of Peter with him. While Stacy was waiting for my return, she saw the boat leave the harbor and she has not been able to reach me since. *Not exactly true after last night when she reached me just fine but Niko didn't need to know that part.*

Does he know were I might be and where is Peter? Niko said he had indeed gone onboard but it was empty so he waited on the back deck for a few minutes and then left. Peter was with him so Stacy must have missed him getting off in the dark. He didn't see anyone else on the boat. Okay, so now we have third party Matt witnessing that Niko says Peter was with him and not on the boat that night. It seems that Niko doesn't know that Peter is dead and may be assuming that Peter is still on the boat with Courtney.

Now for step two. Stacy called Courtney on her cell

phone number. "Courtney," she said, "you don't know me, but Finn Pilar and I have been dating for the last few months."

"Lucky you," Courtney said with more than a little sarcasm.

Stacy didn't rise to the bait but instead said, "I realize it is hard when your ex is dating someone else but Finn only says very nice things about you."

Personally, I thought she laid it on a bit thick.

"What do you want, bitch?" asked Courtney in her best blue blood fashion.

"Well the other night, Finn and I went down to the dock to pick up his GPS from the *Queen Anne's Revenge*. I waited in the bar at Alonzo's and saw your husband and his father go onboard together, then only your father-in-law get off and the boat pulled out of the harbor. This morning I saw you return with the boat but there was no sign of Finn *or* your husband. Do you happen to know what happened to them?"

"Listen, what my husband and I do with our boat, on our time, is none of your business. If you have lost your boyfriend, maybe he is off screwing some other dumb blonde. I'm currently on the boat and he's not here. Besides he's your problem now," and she abruptly hung up.

I smiled at Stacy. "Ok we now have Courtney as much as admitting that Finn and Peter were at least on the boat last night."

My next call was now going to be to Niko Cross. Given that Niko seemed to think that Peter was still on the boat with Courtney and I was not, a call from me to Niko might be a bit of a shock.

"Hey, asshole," I opened. " Iiiiiiiii'm baaaaaaaack."

"Who is this?" he stammered.

"Oh, she told you I was dead and she dumped me over

the side did she?"

Dead air from him.

"Well just so you know, I'm the guy who watched your lover kill her husband, *your son*, and then dump him over the side."

"What the fuck are you talking about?" he choked.

"Oh, she forgot to mention that Peter is dead? Or haven't you talked to her yet?"

I paused for an answer. Dead air again.

"After you and Courtney drugged me, she and Peter took me on a little sea voyage. I am assuming it was to have them dump my body at sea. When I came around after whatever drug you gave me; hell of a hangover by the way, Peter and Courtney were on the back deck arguing. She had a spear gun pointed at him. Suddenly she pulled the trigger and shot him in the chest." I was really enjoying this.

"I figured I would be next so I grabbed the knife she had almost used earlier to cut my throat and used it to cut the cuffs. I went over the side before she could reload the gun. I dove under the boat and came up under swim platform. She just dumped Peter's body, fired up the boat and took off. I rolled onto the swim platform before the boat picked up too much speed and enjoyed a lovely boat ride back to Key West."

I wish I could have had a drone fly over him to see the look on his face.

"Kind of ironic, wouldn't you say? As she drove the boat back to the slip I rolled off and swam ashore. I'll bet she's failed to check in with you yet to let you know she was back and in the harbor as we speak."

More dead air.

"I expect she is going to try and put this on me. She'll probably tell you she doesn't know anything, and that Peter and I were in a fight. I was shot by Peter and she and

Peter came back together, then she dropped him off to report to you when they got back, right?"

More dead air. I was beginning to wonder if there was anybody on the other end of the line.

"Cross, you have tried to kill me twice, once when Squeaky tried to run me down and again on the boat. Not to mention when your boy Georgi tried to shoot me out in the channel."

"So what is your point?" he asked.

"You and Courtney have been running some kind of game with me, Ortega, Linebush, Ransom and Daniels. I suspect you thought you had a partner in her and I think she is just playing everybody. I am just going to sit on the sidelines and watch. Oh, and I'll be telling Ortega he has been played by her as well. Did you know that Ransom is alive as well by the by. She's probably fucking him too."

"I have no idea what you are talking about Pilar but if you know what is good for you, I suggest you make yourself scarce or you could get hurt."

"Go ahead, Cross. Why don't you ask her and see what she says." I hung up.

~ ~ ~

Matt and I hopped in his car and drove over to the harbor. Matt walked over to *Queen Anne's Revenge* and climbed aboard. I went up to Alonzo's to wait. I ordered a Bloody Mary; might as well be comfortable. I called OJ.

"Finn, where the fuck have you been? I have been trying to get you for the last 36 hours."

"I've been busy, what's up?"

I wanted to let you know that the body brought in by Ortega wasn't Eddie Ransom."

"Really?" I feigned surprise.

"It turns out it was Shawn Daniels, the missing CFO."

"No shit, how'd you figure?"

"Listen we need to talk. Where are you?" he asked.

This was a lot easier than I thought. "I am going to be down at the Linebush boat in about a half hour. Why don't you come down there?"

"What? You two back together? That's a shock."

"No way. We have some unfinished business to take care of and you might be able to help. Then we can talk. Oh, and I want it to be a surprise for her, so bring your partner and come on board quietly."

"Finn, what are you up to?" he asked suspiciously.

"Trust me, you will find this interesting." I finished my Bloody Mary and was about to order another when Niko showed up with Georgi at the entrance to the boat slips.

I casually walked up the dock to hear the yelling from about thirty feet away. Matt had Georgi on the deck with a knife at his throat. Matt looked a bit battered but he seemed to have things well in hand.

"You lying bitch!" yelled Niko. "Where the fuck is my son?"

"I told you already." she said, "He came back with me after we dumped Finn and ... "

"Then who the fuck is that?" he pointed at me as I walked up.

She turned and screamed. "You're dead!"

I flashed her my best Mona Lisa smile.

"Boo."

Courtney always had a screw loose but this time she went all the way to full blown wacko. "You can't be alive, you killed Peter," she cried. "I left you for dead twenty-five miles out in the gulf stream two nights ago."

"Would you believe I am a strong swimmer?" I asked.

"Niko, baby, you have to believe me. He killed Peter with a spear gun and then I left him behind in the ocean. There is no way he could have made it back," she whined.

"So Niko, baby," I mimicked her, "If that's the case why didn't she let you know she was back and if I was dead, why didn't she bring back Peter's body rather than leave him for the sharks?"

Matt laughed at that one.

I have to admit, Niko was a pretty tough guy. After a moment to absorb and reflect on the death of his only son, he reached around his back, pulled out a .22 and shot me.

Damn that hurts.

I collapsed on the deck and watched as Matt jumped up and went for the gun. I could only lie there, bleed and wonder why he carried a .22 rather than something bigger. I suppose I should have been grateful because I wasn't dead but damn, it hurt.

Matt had been quick, but still was grazed by the second shot before getting the gun out of Niko's hand and before he was hit from behind with a fire extinguisher by Georgi. He fell to the deck beside me, his eyes rolled back up in his head.

Niko looked over and said to Georgi, "Fire up the boat and release the lines. We need to get out of here NOW!"

The gun had fallen beside me when Matt had grabbed it from Niko. Seeing that both Matt and I were incapacitated, he reached down to pick it up only to find Courtney had picked it up. She pointed it straight at Niko.

"Niko darling, move over to the rail. Georgi, go forward and release the bow lines."

Courtney then turned to me and said, "Finn, sweetie, I have to admit you really did surprise me. I would like to know how you made it back here after I dumped Peter overboard. Clearly I can't leave things to chance again, so I'm going to have to shoot you myself this time." She pointed the gun my way and took aim.

A gun fired as I tried to heroically leap up and wrestle it from her. Well not exactly. More like I cringed and curled up in a ball while wetting my pants. Courtney collapsed like a party balloon that had been hit with a dart and the air whooshed out; sort of a slow fizzle rather than a hard fall.

I opened my eyes in time to see her head hit the deck. A voice shouted, "Freeze", then shots rang out. I felt my vision narrow and a grey curtain shade fell over my eyes. I guess there was a bang then I whimpered.

CHAPTER TWENTY-SIX

I CAME TO with the smiling face of Stacy, holding my hand as we rode in the ambulance to Lower Keys Medical. She had ignored my request and had come down to the docks in time to see the aftermath of the arrests. Georgi had tried to run, or rather swim, after diving off the bow of *Queen Anne's Revenge* but the harbor police made short work picking him up.

Niko was at first defiant, then simply lawyered up. Sadly, Courtney was dead as would I have been, if Niko had used a bigger gun. The Navy SEALs have a saying: 'Never shoot a large caliber man with a small caliber bullet'. *I'm glad Niko was never a SEAL.*

~ ~ ~

The next few days were a blur. Stacy was able to fend off the police and I was given a few days to recover. OJ came by to see how I was doing and brought Crutch for a visit. He seemed indifferent to my plight and after a quick lick he curled up and slept under the hospital bed. A *Service Dog*, Stacy called him. Key West is like that.

Finally, OJ insisted I sit down for an interview in order to try and figure out all that had happened. I walked him through the events on the boat but leaving out my swim ballet with Peter. Niko was claiming that Courtney was raving about how I had killed Peter but could not explain any reason why, other than my jealousy that she had married him after divorcing me. OJ knew that when I thought with the big head, I could give a shit about Courtney so he didn't buy that idea.

Eddie Ransom then shows up claiming that he had been hanging out for the last few days fishing up and down the Lower Keys and did not know that everyone thought he was dead.

I had no proof that Niko tried to have me killed, that he had drugged me and he said that Courtney was the one who shot me. After the hit to the head Matt could not remember Niko as the shooter. In the end, Niko with Peter dead, went back to his now even more lonely mansion out however much money he was owed by Courtney . Ortega was in international waters on *Ciao Bella* by the time anyone thought to have a chat with him. Eddie took over the Linebush companies as executor but with all the family deceased, most of the proceeds went to the state for taxes although surprisingly I inherited $250 thousand dollars from a life insurance policy that Courtney had taken out when we were married and forgotten to change the beneficiary. *Boy was it ever a good thing that OJ shot her. It might have looked like I had a motive.*

The bullet from Niko's .22 had missed any major arteries and after two months of physical therapy, I was back to my regular swims off the beach at Southernmost Café. Stacy and I still see each other but not as often now that she has a job at a law firm in Tampa.

Crutch is now learning a new trick - drinking a shooter from a special bottle of *Doggies's Tequila* at Schooner Wharf.

I expect it will be a real crowd pleaser in the future.

COMING NEXT ...

Yes, you will want to read the next book in the exciting new Finn Pilar mystery series – Tequila Mockingbird.

Here's a sample of this new Key West thriller. The complete edge-of-your-seat adventure will be available soon directly from AbsolutelyAmazingEbooks.com either in paperback or for your favorite e-reader device.

≈≈≈

CHAPTER ONE

They were doing Tequila shots in bed. It was the third round that killed him.

Not a tequila shot, but a .38 caliber one, as they were also playing Russian roulette. I listened to Stacy describe her client and the first thought that went through my head was *natural selection wins again.*

I know that is probably harsh, but I could just picture the scene. "Hey, babe, watch this," as he spun the chamber, and had her put the gun to his head. He took a bite of lime, a salt lick then tossed the tequila and told her to pull the trigger as he came during sex. At least they were playing with a revolver not an automatic. Now that, would be really stupid although with these two it seemed, degrees of stupid is a distinction without much of a difference.

Stacy's call had interrupted my morning exercise routine. I was sitting in the bar at Southernmost Café sipping a Bloody Mary and preparing for my daily swim. Crutch and I had already been on our early morning bike ride around the island. In the case of Crutch, my three-legged dog, it truly is a ride, in the basket.

I have been recovering after my last case and now have only a couple of scars to show for being stabbed, shot and hooked by a fishing gaff trying to survive my crazy ex wife and her gay husband. I know it sounds weird and it was. Stacy my lawyer at the time, then lover for a wonderful two months after the case was over, moved up to Tampa to work at a law firm there. It seems that this client Stacy was calling about was a Key West local who had gone to high school with her and wanted her to handle the case. Stacy was a local girl made good, which could not be said of her client.

As it happened, I knew her client Trixie, a local 'performer' at an adult entertainment emporium known as Pussy Galore. You are safe in assuming it is not a ballroom dancing studio and she was not a contestant on *Dancing with the Stars*. Before you think ill of me, I was not a client of her establishment. She had helped me on a previous case sharing the name of an ex-boyfriend in the drug world. It sounded like her choice of men hadn't improved.

Trixie was apparently doing a bit of crystal meth with her latest beau, the now deceased 'Roco' Ramon. Roco was a three-time loser who she said claimed he was an entrepreneur. I suppose having a small meth lab up on Sugar Loaf Key counts. They were in her trailer on Stock Island just one bridge north of Key West when she pulled out her pair of .45s; D's that is. He also carried a .38. It seems Russian Roulette during sex adds to the rush. They began doing tequila shooters and ultimately .38's. I can't imagine meth, tequila and gunpowder are a good combination but it seemed that Roco had been ingesting too much of the former and ultimately the latter. At least he went out with a bang in more ways than one.

Trixie was brought in for questioning when they found gunpowder residue on her hand. I guess the authorities consider Russian Roulette when someone else pulls the trigger to be murder. She began to sober up and used her call to reach out to Stacy, hence the call to me.

"Trixie is brain dead Finn but she is not a killer. Can you talk to her and see if you can get anything that might help with this case?" she asked.

"Seems pretty open and shut, babe. What are you thinking?"

"It seems that Roco told her he had loaded the gun with a blank so she couldn't be hurt. Having said that, the cops are saying that she owed Roco money for the meth she was using and he was taking it out in trade. She had finally had enough and substituted the blank with a live round. Big difference between premeditated murder and death from misadventure."

"Ok, for you, Stac, anything ... for my usual fee, of course... "

I could hear her snicker and she promised, "Trust me, I miss you too. I will be down there tomorrow and we can ...... debrief."

"I look forward to a wild night of debriefing." I smiled and returned to my Bloody Mary. After a moment's reflection I put in a call to my former partner on the Key West Police force leaving a message asking him to call me.

~ ~ ~

The deep blue waters of the Atlantic Ocean beckoned so I left Crutch in the care of Cindy the bartender and took off on phase three of my daily routine, a swim to the marker and back. It is about thirty minutes and at this time of year the water is warm and the seaweed minimal. As I came in, Cindy had phase four ready for me. *You can't drink all day unless you start in the morning.*

Actually the first Bloody Mary was a virgin, but I have an image to maintain as one of Key West's resident degenerates so I keep that on the down low.

OJ had called back so I redialed and he picked up. "What do you need, Dude?" he growled

"I just needed to hear your happy voice on this fine day." I said disingenuously.

"Bullshit, Finn, you only call when you need something and it is always a fine day on 'The Rock'."

"OJ, that's why you are a detective. Because of your breathtaking insight." I smiled.

"Fuck off, Finn," and he hung up. People are always hanging up on me.

OJ and I had been partners when I served on the Key West Police Department for eight years. After I was 'retired' by the city at the encouragement of my then soon to be ex father-in-law, I felt sorry for myself. My wife, but soon to be ex-wife, had grown disenchanted with me after I help put her brother in prison for running a Ponzi scheme involving a local marina.

I was virtually broke with a small pension from the city (read they bought me off for $50k) which is about enough to pay a Key West bar tab for a year.

For the first 6 months I did my best to put a dint in it at my favorite rum bar. I was divorced, out of a job, broke and about to get kicked out of my apartment. "Apartment" is a bit of hyperbole given that it was a room in a small conch cottage, owned by a retiree who needed extra money.

After a particularly abusive weekend Bahama Bob, my favorite bartender at the Rum Bar, called a friend of mine and told him I was in need of a little intervention. Matt Divine was a former BUD/S instructor when I was in the Navy SEAL program. Even though I was a DOR or Drop on Request during second phase due to injuries, we remained in touch and over time became friends. Matt runs an insurance investigation firm in Miami and he came down to the 'Rock', got me dried out, lent me the money to buy a small Shotgun cottage in Old Town Key West and got me working again doing run of the mill claims disputes in the Keys.

I ended up working on a big case involving my ex-wife, her family and another old line Key West 'Bubbas'. Bubbas are the locally born and raised Key West aristocrats, the small town big shots who are a little inbred and like to think they run the show. Courtney my ex, ended up being shot and killed by my ex partner, and no not that kind of partner and I inherited $250k from a forgotten insurance policy.

The money had been burning a hole in my pocket and last month I was approached by an old accounting buddy of mine about investing in a bar he was setting up in the old Key West Pub location on Duval near Southernmost Point. He needed $100K to build out the leasehold improvements on the place and asked if I was interested in investing. Thomas A. Finch and I worked at a small accounting firm in San Diego together before I went into the Navy but nobody called him Tom. Given his last name and his accounting degree everyone called him 'Abacus'.

After discussing the idea with Matt and given that I lived around the corner from the site, I decided owning a local bar was not a bad idea. Abacus explained his concept and I was in. We were going to be the proud owners of the newest Key West bar and grill 'The Mockingbird'. *I imagine you can guess what drinks we were going to feature ....*

Thank you for reading.
Please review this book. Reviews help others find
Absolutely Amazing eBooks and inspire us to keep
providing these marvelous tales.

If you would like to be put on our email list to receive
updates on new releases, contests, and promotions, please
go to AbsolutelyAmazingEbooks.com and sign up.

About the Author

Lewis C. Haskell is a former international corporate executive and today is a fresh water conch who has owned property in Key West for 15 years. A diver, sailor, and Harley owner, he can be found riding his bicycle around town most mornings or with a glass of wine at Grand Vin in the evening.

ABSOLUTELY AMAZING eBOOKS

AbsolutelyAmazingEbooks.com
or AA-eBooks.com

Made in the USA
Charleston, SC
30 December 2015